TOMB SONG

TOMB SONG

A NOVEL

Julián Herbert

Translated from the Spanish by
Christina MacSweeney

Graywolf Press

The author would like to thank his friends Mabel Garza and Mario Zertuche for their hospitality in Lamadrid, Coahuila, Mexico.

This publication is made possible, in part, by the voters of Minnesota through a Minnesota State Arts Board Operating Support grant, thanks to a legislative appropriation from the arts and cultural heritage fund, and a grant from the Wells Fargo Foundation. Significant support has also been provided by Target, the McKnight Foundation, the Lannan Foundation, the Amazon Literary Partnership, and other generous contributions from foundations, corporations, and individuals. To these organizations and individuals we offer our heartfelt thanks.

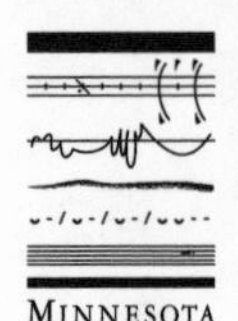

Published by Graywolf Press
250 Third Avenue North, Suite 600
Minneapolis, Minnesota 55401

www.graywolfpress.org

Published in the United States of America
Printed in Canada

ISBN 978-1-55597-799-3

2 4 6 8 9 7 5 3 1
First Graywolf Printing, 2018

Library of Congress Control Number: 2017938026

Cover design: Walter Green

To Mónica

There's only one mother. And I got her.

Armando J. Guerra

Contents

As a child, I wanted to be a scientist or a doctor. A man in a white coat. But all too soon I discovered my lack of aptitude: it took me years to accept the roundness of the earth. In public, I faked it. Once, in a classroom (one of many, as I went to nine different primary schools), without a hint of stage fright, I gave a visual demonstration of the terms *rotation* and *orbit* using—as the textbook suggested—an orange decorated with blue crayon and pierced by my pencil. I memorized every illusory story, the segments captured in midrotation, the hours and days, the transit of the sun . . . But inside, no, I didn't believe any of it. I lived with the proud, lucid anguish that had caused so many heresiarchs to be flayed to death at the orders of Saint Augustine.

It was Mamá's fault. We traveled so much that, for me, the earth was a wickerwork polygon limited in every direction by railway lines. Curved, straight, circular, overhead, underground tracks. Ferrous but tenuous atmospheres, like something from a disaster movie where icebergs crash into each other. Boundaries as transitional as a tunnel, sheer as a cliff in the Copper Canyon, crisp as a field of alfalfa in which the railway sleepers tap out their dance as the trains pass over. Sometimes, atop a rock or perched on a high point of a headland on the Acapulco coast, I'd look out to sea and believe I could spot yellow wagons and diesel locomotives with the insignia *N de M* rattling along, ghostly, beyond the breeze. Sometimes, at night, from a window, I'd pretend the fireflies below the bridge were those neighboring galaxies my older brother used to talk about. Sometimes, while I was sleeping in a moving metal corridor, hugging unknown children, or standing in a press of bodies smelling of fresh sorghum and four-day-old sweat, or with my bones hunched up on hard wooden seats, I dreamed that the form and substance of the planet was changing by the second. One afternoon, while the train was going through a classification yard in Paredón, I decided that the whistle of the locomotive was announcing our arrival at the end of the world.

That's all stupid, of course. It makes me feel horribly sad. Especially now, as I watch Mamá lying motionless on a hospital bed—her strength gone, her arms covered in bruises from the needles—connected to the blood-splattered, translucent IV tubing, transformed into a chemical map by means of misspelled entries written in ballpoint pen, identifying the poisons they're injecting into her: Tempra, 1 gram, ceftazidime, cytarabine, anthracycline, ciprofloxacin, doxorubicin, 1,000 cc mixed solutions cloaked in black plastic to protect the venom from the light. Crying because her best-loved and most-hated son (the only one who had ever been able to save her from her nightmares, the only one to whom she had shouted, "You're not my son anymore, you bastard, you're nothing but a mad dog") has to spoon-feed her and see her shriveled nipples when he changes her gown, has to carry her to the bathroom and hear—and smell: and she hates the stink so much—her shit. Weak. Drunk from three transfusions. Awaiting, behind the defenses of her face mask, another bone marrow test. I'm sorry not to have been, because of her—because of her hysterical life crisscrossing the whole blessed country in search of a house or a lover or a job or happiness, none of which have ever existed in this Sweet Nation—a model child: a child capable of believing in the roundness of the earth. Someone who could have explained something to her; prescribed something for her. Someone capable of consoling her by means of an oracle of rational putrefaction in this hour when her body shudders, gasping for breath and fearing death.

I

"I DON'T FUCKIN' CARE ABOUT SPIRITUALITY"

Mamá was born on December 12, 1942, in the city of San Luis Potosí. As so often happens, she was named after a virgin: Guadalupe. Guadalupe Chávez Moreno. However, she assumed a large number of aliases during her lifetime—both to give herself an air of mystery, and because she views her existence as a criminal event. She changed names with the nonchalance with which other women dye or perm their hair. Sometimes, when she took her children to visit her narco friends in Nueva Italia, or the old spinsters of Irapuato for whom she worked as a servant after running away from my grandmother's house in Monterrey (there's a photo: she's fourteen years old, her hair is close-cropped, and she's wearing a blouse with an appliqué design she'd sewn on herself), or the short-lived aunts-by-marriage in Matamoros, Lázaro Cárdenas, or Villa de la Paz, she'd instruct us:

"I'm called Lorena Menchaca here, and I'm a cousin of the Karate Teacher."

"My name's Vicky here."

"Here I'm called Juana, just like your grandma."

(My grandmother, for the most part, called her Damned Wretch while she dragged her around the yard by the hair, smashing her face into the plant pots.)

The most enduring of these identities was Marisela Acosta. For years, under this name, my mother worked in the prostitution industry.

That pseudonym contains a smidgeon of truth. Guadalupe's biological father was called Pedro Acosta. He was a musician (there's a photo: he's standing in front of his group, Son Borincano, with my great-uncle Juan—brother of my grandmother Juana—playing a tresillo guitar) who, the story goes, eventually owned a chain of grocery stores in La Merced. Mamá didn't know him well. She may have met him once, but what's more likely is that she never did, and didn't give him a moment's thought either. The man who accepted her as his daughter was a stepfather: my grandfather Marcelino Chávez.

I don't know exactly when she became Marisela; that's what she was called when I was old enough to be aware of her as an individual. She was very beautiful: small and slim, her straight hair hanging down to her waist, a firm body and unashamedly resplendent indigenous features. Although she was past thirty, she looked much younger. A real sexpot: to make the most of her wide hips, round buttocks, and flat stomach, she'd wear jeans with a long scarf wrapped crosswise over her small breasts and knotted at the back.

Some days she'd tie her hair up in a ponytail, put on dark glasses, and lead me by the hand through the lackluster streets of Acapulco's red-light district, the Zona de Tolerancia, to the market stalls on the avenue by the canal (this would have been eight or nine in the morning, when the last drunkards were leaving La Huerta or Pepe Carioca, and women wrapped in towels would lean out over the metal windowsills of tiny rooms and call me "pretty"). With the exquisite abandon and spleen of a whore who's been up all night, she'd buy me a Choco Milk shake and two coloring books.

All the men watching her.

But she was with me.

At the age of five, I first experienced the masochistic pleasure of coveting something you own but can't understand.

It seems to me now that Mamá had one very good and one very bad eye when it came to choosing her gentlemen friends. I remember there was an Italian, Renato: he bought me a puppet dressed in a mariachi outfit. I remember a certain Eliezur—I rechristened him Eldeazure—who once took us to Choya the Clown's circus. She never spoke about them. Not to me, I mean. The only method I have for evaluating her love life is to observe it through the lens of her offspring, each child by a different father.

My elder sister, Adriana, is the bastard daughter of Isaac Valverde, an exceptional businessman and pimp, part owner of a fabled brothel: La Huerta.

La Huerta was on the other side of the canal. The premises stretched over perhaps half a block. It could have been the opium dream of any wealthy old man unafraid of catching dysentery or venereal disease. Even back in the seventies, it had personal reserved parking spaces, private security, and three or four salons specializing in the diverse proclivities of their clientele scattered between the mango trees and coconut palms. I never knew exactly what those proclivities were, and I daresay I can live without that knowledge. There was also a bar and a restaurant, water that was almost fit to drink, and a long, high redbrick wall—without any neon signs on the outside—that snaked along as far as the edge of Callejón Mal Paso. A wall that left you the victim of cliché since it produced the sensation of bordering a medieval fortress. It was the primitive Acapulco crossover, a labyrinth/laboratory of what Mexico is today for the American Way of Life: a gigantic, pseudoexotic whorehouse with the infrastructure of a gringo suburb, full of cheap bodies with assholes you can stick your finger in before dragging their human flesh to the other side of the wall. Once, while we were walking by that brick wall, Marisela said, "Lobo y Melón used to play here." I knew—as would any child who'd grown up in the vicinity of a brothel—that behind that bulwark the revolver of sex was camped out. And I had the vague notion that from sex sprung a volatile mortification of the flesh that mingled with ordinary things: money, the tumult of the night, and the silence of the day. Apart from that elusive, squalid insight, I didn't understand a damn thing. But thanks to Mamá's comment, years later I managed to associate sex with music, that other force of nature that has been scything misfortune with sweeps of the machete since the days of Stromberg-Carlson radios.

My older brother is the son of a *madrina*—a sort of unofficial police spy—in Monterrey who, by the early eighties, had become Commander Jorge Fernández, head of the investigative unit of the crime prevention squad. They say he wasn't the type to be cowed by anyone. He was killed in a drug raid some fifteen years ago. Jorge junior had seen him only sporadically. On one of those occasions, when my brother was fourteen, the commander gave him a motorbike.

My younger brother came from the other extreme. Saíd was the son of Don B, a Monterrey goodfella of not particularly high standing, but who was much loved in the profession. Even now, Don B is one of those decadent outlaws who have their photos taken with the Western film actors Fernando and Mario Almada. He was an exceptionally handsome man—a trait my brother inherited—and in his younger days his talent for doling out beatings was notorious. He never, however, laid a hand on my mother. My childhood memories have him buying me toys and treating me with more unadulterated affection than I ever received from any other adult man. He's something like a platonic father to me. Mamá claims I picked him out for her because I started calling him "Papá" before they became lovers. It's been more than twenty years since I last saw him. A few weeks ago, he sent me an Aldo Conti suit, accompanied by a note: "For my son, El Cacho." I never wear suits. And it didn't fit, either.

At the beginning of the eighties, Mamá had a daughter with Armando Rica, a session drummer nicknamed La Calilla for his muscular physique. He never saw Diana, my little sister: he lived in such an unremitting state of depression that, after a lover's quarrel, he filled his belly with barbiturates. The neighbors found him. They say he was trying to say something into the microphone of a tape recorder and froth spewed out of his mouth. Mamá, in one of her classic fits of gypsy hysteria, had fled—I'm not sure if it was to Coatzacoalcos or Reynosa—leaving behind both her pimp and her children. By the time she came back to Monterrey, La Calilla was rotting in a cemetery and we owed money everywhere.

I'm the middle son. My father, Gilberto Membreño, is the least spectacular boyfriend Marisela ever had. He started out as a delivery boy in a drugstore but ended up as the sales manager of several establishments belonging to the Meliá hotel chain. In 1999, with his judgment destroyed by Chivas Regal whiskey and Sauza Hornitos tequila, he attempted to remake himself as a playboy: he packed in his job, married Marta (a Colombian girl of my own age), bought a 1965 Mustang, and launched a business that went bankrupt in less than a year. I haven't seen him since.

As I complete this list, I feel ashamed. Not for narrating embarrassing personal matters: but because my literary technique is lamentable and the events I want to recall have a veneer of stunning implausibility. I'm in room 101 of the Saltillo University Hospital, writing in the near dark. Writing with my fingers in the door. My main character is lying wrecked on the bed due to acute myeloid leukemia (AML, as the doctors call it) while I compile her most ridiculous variations. Her frowning face in the shadows tacitly reproves the glimmer of my laptop as, in her sleep, she perhaps longs for the asexualized love of her children.

Some time ago, at a cocktail party in Sant Joan de les Abadesses, a Mexican poet and diplomat said to me:

"I read the biographical note that accompanied a story of yours in an anthology. I found it entertaining but obscene. I can't work out why you would want to pretend such a terrifying piece of fiction is or ever was *real*."

Such observations make me pessimistic about the future of narrative art. We read nothing, and we demand that nothing lack nuances of either the ordinary or the sublime. And what's worse: demand it be ordinary without cliché, sublime without any unexpected change of accent. Aseptically literary. Efficient to the point of frigidity. In the majority of cases, a postmodern novel is nothing more than *costumbrismo* cross-dressing as cool jazz and/or pedantic rhetoric à la Kenneth Goldsmith that spends a hundred pages saying what Baudelaire said in three words: *spleen et ideal*.

"Technique, my boy," says a voice in my head. "Shuffle the technique."

To hell with it: in her youth, Mamá was a beautiful half-breed Indian who had five husbands: a fabled pimp, a police officer riddled with bullet holes, a splendid goodfella, a suicidal musician, and a pathetic Humphrey Bogart impersonator. PERIOD.

Her last partner dates from the early nineties. We'd only just moved to Saltillo (this city in which, now, while day is breaking, instead of birdsong, I hear the murmur of the infusion pumps that rule the hospital) when she got involved with Margarito J. Hernández. Journalist. Alcoholic. Ugly. It didn't last long. Mamá didn't love him.

Margarito gave me my first real job: copyediting at a corrupt political magazine. I was seventeen. One day, he offered me some advice:

"Just say fuck it all and get out of Mexico. Because you're

going to be a writer. And in this country, a writer is no good for anything; he's dead weight."

In her midfifties, Marisela decided to accept that she was alone. Her three older children had stopped speaking to her. She had no friends. Not even her daughters-in-law or grandchildren came to visit her. She fractured three bones in the course of a few months. In 1997 she was diagnosed with severe osteoporosis. Little by little, as if unwillingly, she began to use her real name: Guadalupe Chávez Moreno. Spanking new, freshly extracted from the repository of her childhood.

What none of us knew was that, after undertaking that symbolic renunciation of her fantasy of being Other, Mamá had also decided to grow old. She never got to be an adult. It took fewer than ten years for her to pass from morbid adolescence to premature senility. And that record—or better still: that bad habit—is the only inheritance she will leave her children.

I leave the hospital after my first thirty-six-hour shift. Mónica comes to pick me up. The light of the real world feels brutal: coarse powdered milk made atmosphere. Mónica asks me to save all the bills in case the medical expenses are tax deductible. She adds that my former employer promised the cultural institute would cover part of the cost. And that Maruca has been behaving well but is missing me dreadfully. That the garden, the ceiba tree, and the jacaranda have been recently watered. Not a word she says gets through to me: I can't make the emotional connection. I say yes to everything. Exhaustion. It would need the skill of a tightrope walker and the frenzy of an unbalanced mind to doze in a chair without armrests, far from the wall and close to the reggaeton playing on the radio in the nurses' station: Du-du-do you dare come out of the closet sh-sh-show yerself take off the varnish stop clothin' yerself cos the one who's gonna paint you is yerself. A voice in my head woke me up in the early hours. It was saying: "Don't be afraid. Nothing that's yours comes from you." I kneaded the back of my neck and closed my eyes: I thought it must be a huckster koan read out by the fortune-teller Mizada Mohamed coming from the television in the next room. It's not reality that makes a person cynical. It's the near impossibility of getting any sleep in cities.

We arrive back home. Mónica opens the front gate, puts away the Atos, and says:

"After lunch, if you feel up to it, come into the garden for a while to read in the sun. It's always good news when the sun comes out."

I'd like to tease my wife for uttering such banalities. But I don't have the energy. And anyway, the sun falls with palpable bliss on my cheeks, on the recently watered lawn, on the leaves of the jacaranda . . . I collapse onto the grass. Maruca, our dog, comes bounding out to greet me. I close my eyes. Cynicism requires rhetoric. Sitting in the sun doesn't.

When she was admitted through the emergency room, someone misspelled her name: Guadalupe "Charles." That's what they all call her in the hospital. Guadalupe Charles. Every so often, in the darkness, when I'm most afraid, I try to convince myself I'm watching over the delirium of a stranger.

After a thousand failed attempts—Google searches, e-mails, Skype, and long-distance telephone calls to nonexistent accounts and numbers one digit short—Mónica tracks down my elder brother on a mobile phone with the area code for Yokohama, Japan. Would he call me? I answer. Solemn, without greeting me, Jorge asks:

"Is everyone at her bedside . . . ? You have to be there with her in these difficult days."

I suppose he's lived abroad for so long he's ended up swallowing the exotic pill of advertising via the Abuelita cocoa powder slogan: There's-No-Greater-Love-Than-the-Love-of-the-Great-Mexican-Family. I say no. Saíd is a mess and no doubt hooked on something or other; in his state, he isn't up to the stress of a hospital. Mónica is doing her part outside (I'd like to say "in the outside world," but today, for me, the outside world is immeasurable: hyperspace) as Director of Communications and Logistics of My Mother's Leukemia. Diana has two babies and can manage a shift only every other night. Adriana is lost to the world: she left home when I was seven, so I hardly even know her. I've seen her no more than a couple of times in my adult life. The last was in 1994.

"For the past week, I've been doing thirty-six-hour shifts, dozing or writing by the bed of a dying woman," I add melodramatically.

What I don't add is: Welcome to the Apache nation. Eat your children if you don't want the Palefaces, those white trash, to corrupt them. The only Family that gets along in this country is a narcotrafficking clan in Michoacán that cuts off people's heads. Jorge, Jorgito, hello: the Great Mexican Family came tumbling down like a pile of stones, Pedro Páramo dissolving under his illegitimate son Abundio's knife before the startled eyes of Damiana, the Televisa model who goes on robotically repeating: Coming to you from Lake Celestún, this is XEW . . . Nothing: there's nothing left but pure, shitty, cunty nothingness. In this Sweet Nation where my mother is dying, not a single sheet of *papel picado* is left. Not a shot of tequila uncorrupted by the perfume of marketing. Not even a speck of sadness or decency or an outcry that hasn't been branded by the ghost of an AK-47.

Two nights before we took Mamá to the hospital, Mónica dreamed we were constructing a swimming pool beside the fig tree in our garden. The rubble we hauled away in wheelbarrows wasn't dirt or rocks: it was human thighs. That's weird, I said, I wasn't going to tell you, but I dreamed they closed down the elevated section of the Periférico beltway because a truck loaded with giant heads—like the one in that hyperrealistic self-portrait by Ron Mueck—had overturned. The eyes of the heads were open and the hair soaked in blood.

(During breakfast, Felipe Calderón Hinojosa comes on the TV to inform the nation of the achievements of his government, whose inflated statistics he—obviously—considers to be more relevant than a hundred thousand nightmares.)

"Have you prepared yourself . . . ?" Jorge asks, and adds, "It's natural. Don't let it get you down. It's the cycle of life."

As if I was in any condition for clichés. I remember a prophetic line by Juan Carlos Bautista: "Heads will rain down on Mexico." Was he talking about the hostages executed in La

Marquesa in 2008? Or Ron Mueck's self-portrait? Was he talking about my mamá's leukemia . . . ? Heads will rain down on Mexico. What planet does this Japanese guy who shares my surname live on? Of course I'm prepared; did the Family leave me any other choice?

Every household runs aground at the feet of a domestic myth. It can be anything: educational excellence or a passion for soccer. I grew up in the shadow of a turn of the screw: the pretense that mine really was a family.

Jorge left home when I was thirteen. I have no memory of him before I was three. (It was Chesterton who said that the story of his birth had been handed down to him through oral tradition, and so could be wrong.) That leaves us a margin of ten shared years. However, Mamá wasn't content to flit from place to place: usually one of her children (very often me; years later, my younger sister) was chosen to accompany her on her railroad orgies. Meanwhile, the others were left with family members and/or in the homes of "reliable women": atrocious, gruff grannies who taught us to love Charles Dickens in Indian Territory. There was a Señora Amparo from Monterrey who recommended I start getting used to things because when I grew up I was going to be a faggot. She said this to rid herself, in advance, of her sense of guilt for the intrepid attempts her eldest son made to rape me. In Querétaro, there was a Doña Duve who, hoping to hang on to Saíd for good (being the best looking and youngest, he was her pet), held him hostage for four days in an attic, eating and sleeping on the floor, with one ankle shackled to a rail. Another woman, in Monclova, forced us to stop using our childhood nicknames (Coco, Cachito, Pumita) on pain of being caned on the buttocks.

I'm sure that such mistreatment wasn't simple cruelty. In part, it resulted from the frustration of weeks going by without Mamá managing to pay our keep.

So I'd lived under the same roof as Jorge—this Nippon guy who embodies the most sacred paternal figure I'll ever know—for scarcely seven years, plus the odd summer holiday. He's over forty now. I'm nearly thirty-eight. And I'm supposed to write him a letter that begins: "Sadly, the diagnosis has been confirmed: Lupita has leukemia. I am sorry to be the bearer of this news without also being able to give you a hug."

(With Jorge, I always call her *Lupita.* Not to distance myself from her: to distance myself from him. How do you tell an almost unknown foreigner that his mother, your mother, is dying . . . ?)

After the initial circumlocution, I go on to ask him for money. I finish the letter and send it by e-mail. I shut down my laptop, leave the hospital with Mónica. We have an hour and a half to eat. We go to a Vips restaurant.

"Could you tell me which dish takes the least time to prepare?" she asks.

"Of course, señorita. We're at your service. What can I get you?"

"The quickest dish on the menu, please."

"Well . . . I'd suggest the grilled chicken breast. Or the marinated beefsteak with tortilla chips. We have several kinds of hamburgers, all very tasty. Or do you want a light meal? We have a lite menu. And there's the *mole* assortment, four different var . . . No . . . ? Of course, señorita. But while you're waiting, can I offer you a starter? How about a spring roll? Would you like to order your dessert . . . ?"

The food takes forever to arrive. Two waitresses, an underling, and the baby-faced assistant manager come to our table and offer us intoxicating apologies. Can you imagine such a scene in Paris or La Habana . . . ? Of course not. Which just goes to show, among other things, that the Mexican Revolution was a fiasco: the main aim of true revolutions is to turn waiters into bad-mannered despots.

By the time the dishes finally appear on the table, both Mo and I are in a terrible mood. We don't enjoy the food. We rush to finish. While I'm paying the bill, the woman at the cash register is over-the-top polite and asks us, if it isn't too much trouble, to fill out a questionnaire, the only objective of which is to improve every day on the service the company offers, always striving, of course, for excellence. She points to two metal plaques on the wall: "Mission" and "Vision." Once again the omni-incompetent, ostentatious Mexican-style ISO 9000 quality-control system greeting us with an obscene eulogy to Carlos Slim, freshly washed in the dysfunctional bathrooms of fifty million undernourished people. The whole of Mexico is the territory of the cruel.

Suddenly, I see myself clearly: I'm just the same. This restaurant service is a metaphor for the letter I've just written to my Japanese brother. I'm a waiter in a country of waiters. Some of my fellow workers have appeared in *Forbes Magazine*, while others are content to wear a tricolor sash on their chest. It makes no difference: here, all of us waiters uphold the civil code of spitting in your soup. First we waste your time with our proverbial courtesy; then we waste it with criminal stupidity.

Welcome to the Sweet Nation.

Tip, please.

Mamá Calavera

Once, on the Day of the Dead, I dreamed my mother was the skeletal figure of the *calaca*. We'd crossed half of Michoacán State: Uruapan, Playa Azul, Nueva Italia, Venustiano Carranza, Santa Clara, Paracho . . . We'd stayed in phantasmal hotels. In the uncomfortable cabin of a truck. In semiderelict houses with only an oil lamp for illumination. It wasn't tourism, it wasn't altruism; we were part of the fanatical fan club that followed in the wake of a glorious team in danger of extinction: the Balsas Larks. A soccer club that counted among its ranks Garras, Chaparro Mel, Eldeazul, Torre Mijares, and El Cyclón. Barmen and waiters from the brothel in the city of Lázaro Cárdenas where my mother earned her living.

Someone told us—this was years before the engineer Cuauhtémoc Cárdenas assumed the state governorship for the PRI and ruined my childhood with the implementation of a bilious prohibition law—business was booming in that city thanks to the new highway and the peak in demand for steel, the benefits of which were pouring down on the Truchas steelworks. Hundreds of workmen, recently uprooted from the mountains of Guerrero and Oaxaca, were paying nervous visits, at all hours of the day and night, to the whorehouses: disillusioned former guerrillas, and army deserters, and fugitives from the copra or poppy harvests, who one fine day found themselves, for the first time, in possession of low-risk jobs, decent wages, and fat year-end bonuses.

Mamá and I moved from Querétaro to Lázaro Cárdenas to check it out, provisionally leaving my siblings in the care of Señora Duve. As we didn't have enough to pay someone to care for me, or to take a house, Mamá persuaded the manager of the brothel to let me secretly live in the small room she rented at the back of the premises. To assuage this man's conscience, she had to promise—as if the place were not a whorehouse, but a pension for young ladies—she would never allow men in there.

My mother kept office hours: she worked five eight-hour shifts a week. From ten at night to six in the morning. From Tuesday night to dawn on Sunday. She never earned much. Her income came from ticketing dances and drinks. She always boasted of being a prostitute with a cast-iron code, and her principal rule consisted of not having intercourse in exchange for money ("I dance," she would say when, well and truly plastered, she'd ask our forgiveness; "I dance" and, as if we were babies incapable of understanding her words, she'd mime the movement of her hips, one hand on her belly and the other in the air, near her ear). Nowadays, I think it was an inopportune, even impractical, rule. I suppose, however, more than an exercise of morality and good manners, what underlay her ethic was the leftovers of militant unionism inherited from my grandfather Marcelino, who was active in the railways movement at the end of the fifties.

Mamá would return to our room at dawn. Generally drunk. She'd hug me close to her chest and try to sleep for a few hours. I'd wait until I heard her snoring to slip from between her long-nailed hands, through the metal door, trying to keep it from squeaking, then dodge a scolding from the caretaker and the presence of the other shrill, heavily made-up women whose shouts and obscenities could be heard behind the series of doors leading into the fornication rooms: *you frigging evil whore, balls-loving nympho born of a soft prick, the way you are you cocksucker yer only fit for washing a pussy.* I'd walk along the narrow corridor running down one side of the building to the street, or rather to the vacant lot surrounded by a chain-link fence next to the brothel. A parking lot (empty of cars at that hour of the day) the barmen and waiters—black shadows under their eyes and bathed in sweat—would daily use as an improvised virtuous soccer pitch.

At first none of them were keen to have me there as a spectator. The moment they spotted me, the players would cease hostilities to inform the manager the bastard kid of the Mary—as the women were known—was spying on them again. The manager would wake Mamá and threaten to kick us out. Mamá would take me back to the room, refusing to allow herself to cry, and no doubt feeling like slapping me. All she'd say was:

"Child, please be good, look after me while I'm asleep. Can't you see I'm alone . . . ?"

I didn't obey her.

Eventually, since I never interrupted the play (a soccer match with time-outs is an Asian scroll reduced to a Hallmark card), the players resigned themselves to having me as an audience. To cover up my illicit presence, the manager would end up standing beside me to watch the game. Later, some women—my mother among them—would appear now and again around the chain-link fence. It wasn't long before the cheering-on, betting, and early-morning beers began.

One day Chaparro Mel went to see the manager with a communal petition:

"We're ready, boss. We've done the practice, and now we want you to sponsor our application for the municipal league."

And so the Zombie Larks were born (Zombie was the alias

of the establishment). In his role as patriarch, the manager forked out for the enrollment fee, the photos of their credentials, and a beautiful cherry-red and white uniform that came apart at the seams every game. El Ciclón sought out my mother one afternoon and explained (from the corridor, of course) that, as I was always hanging around, and was a supporter, he'd put my name forward as the team mascot. It was a pretext for getting off with her. But I didn't care: I only remember the feverish excitement of standing in front of the mirror dressed in my first soccer uniform.

The Larks won the municipal championship. They had what it took to steamroll their way through: strict daily practice at an early hour, an unhealthy determination to shine at something, an almost total ban on drinking in the evenings, disciplined rage, the ability to lay traps as a team . . . They also, of course, had the most provocative, disconcerting fan base in the competition.

Flush with success, they exercised their right as champions (a right the local authorities attempted to retract by all possible means, offended by the idea that Lázaro Cárdenas would play against the rest of Michoacán State represented by a bunch of pickpockets, bouncers, and pimps) to enlist in the state league. And to make matters even worse, they changed their name to the Balsas Larks.

"Well, now you don't just represent a humble bordello," declaimed the manager during an elegant ceremony around the dive's bar, "but also the Balsas itself, the wide river that runs on one flank of our beloved city, alongside the largest and most prosperous steelworks in Mexico."

As so often happens in this country, after the best speeches of the president of the day, it was all downhill from there.

The Larks belatedly discovered that to excel at the state level you need serious patronage: money. They had to travel twice a month to away games, which meant missing work and, therefore, lost tips. They didn't always have to go far, but Michoacán is a big state: trips could take four or five hours. Food had to be bought and the gas and overnight accommodation paid for. It was no easy task to find lodgings for thirteen or fourteen people in some of the smaller towns. And then there were always the distrustful ranchers prepared to pull out their Magnums first and ask questions later if anyone accidentally trespassed into the clandestine areas of their property.

Another complication had to do with transportation logistics. When they lost a match, mutual recriminations meant certain players had to be kept apart at all costs on the way back. If they won, at least one large, easily handled vehicle with a good engine was a must since the local fans, accustomed to the "Law of the Sierra," didn't do things by half . . . Gobs of spit, water bombs, farts, and thrown bottles were never in short supply. And one spectator would inevitably feel the urge to get out his machete and feign a swipe at our center forward.

At local tournaments, things were even worse. Without the support of the municipal league or any other of the city's teams (after all, they had humiliated bank executives, blast furnace operators, and graduates of the Monterrey Tech on the field), the Larks often had no home field. On one occasion they even went so far as to improvise a one-off match in the parking lot where they trained, using buckets to mark the goalposts. The state sports body fined them and adjudged the game to be lost by default.

The cash ran out. The fans evaporated. The players gradually deserted the team. Sometimes we were a man short and had to bribe the ref not to call the game. My mother and I were their most committed supporters. She understood what the team meant for me and backed me to the hilt.

Then the final match of the year came around. We took to

the pitch in Maldemillares, a community of just a few hundred inhabitants. It was a depressing, empty shell of a game; since we knew the team had already been disqualified, it was just a matter of going through the motions of playing the final fixture on the sporting calendar. Not even I had the enthusiasm to cheer or kiss the shirt of my soiled uniform. The match ended in a 3–1 defeat. Knowing our position in the standings, the locals took pity on us: we were invited to the town fiesta.

It was November 2, the Day of the Dead. Despite the fact that it was in Michoacán, the festivity didn't resemble any of those braggadocio, schizofolkloric affairs you're saddled with in state schools: no mortuary altars, candles, plates of tamales, or little salt crucifixes. Instead of all that, it was children with Chicano accents trick-or-treating between the maize fields and the stables, old women saying the rosary with their faces covered with black rebozos and Avon cosmetics, and men in Ramblers smoking reefer or drinking cane sugar liquor to the sound of Led Zeppelin or Los Cadetes de Linares . . .

I don't remember having seen the sugar skulls with names on their foreheads before, but they really were amazing. El Ciclón, creep that he was, brought my mother one that said "Mary." I got jealous. As a consolation, Mamá treated me to one of the sugar candies. Spurred on by a little rage and a little more greed, I popped the whole thing in my mouth and pulverized it with two chomps. It tasted awful. Like an injection. I mean: like the smell of alcohol on the gauze they used to wipe across my buttocks before vaccinations.

We returned to Lázaro that night, flopped in the back of a pickup. Some of the Larks were quietly singing a song by Rigo Tovar: wherever you've gone, woman, you won't find another love like this.

The murmur of their voices lulled me to sleep.

I dreamed I was one of them. I dreamed my mother kissed

me on the lips. She smoothed my hair and said, "Go to sleep now." She caressed me with her slender hands, with the tips of her long dark-purple nails, with her phosphorus-white hands, her hands that drew sparks from the darkness. I ran my fingers up her arm until I reached her shoulder, her neck, her face: all soft, all pale, all bone. Mamá was a hard, white *calavera*, smelling of vaccinations. A Halloween ghost, a sugar skeleton with hair.

I woke with a start, crying among the singers. Mamá wanted to give me a hug, but even with my eyes open, I could still see the face of death in her face. I tried to pull away from her and jump out of the pickup. Marisela clasped both arms around me and pressed me to her chest. She calmed me. She reminded me who she was. Repeated it several times:

"It's me, Cachito. I'm your mommy."

Alerted by the other passengers, the driver braked. We stopped for a while at a bend in the road, and I gradually managed to calm down. I asked Marisela to let me see her face clearly, to check she wasn't the skeletal figure of La Huesuda. We were in the shadows, so one of the players took out his lighter and lit up her face with the flame.

"See?" she said in a calming voice. "It's me. Same as usual: with my flesh, and my ears, and my hair."

I gave a sigh of relief and hugged her waist. We restarted our journey; the travelers began to sing again. This time it was a song by Camilo Sesto: living is dying of love, from love my soul is wounded.

That was the last match the Balsas Larks ever played.

When we got back to the Zombie, Mamá pulled back the covers of the bed, bathed and cradled me. Then she took a shower and began to put on her makeup to go to work, if only for a short while. I spied on her, my eyes half closed, pretending to be asleep. I wondered if her skin might not be just one more layer of paint, powder, cream, and the other unguents she was now applying to her eyelids, cheeks, and lips. Just like in *The Invaders*, the TV show in which aliens disguise themselves as earthlings: “David Vincent has seen them . . .” I wondered if my mother, under all those products, might not be death herself: the *calavera* of my dreams.

Mamá Retórica

What I'm writing is a work of suspense. Not in its technique: in its poetics. Not for you, but for me. What will become of these pages if my mother doesn't die?

I've endeavored to draw a freehand portrait of my leukemic mother. A portrait garnished with childhood reminiscence, biographical detail, and the occasional dash of fiction. It's a portrait (a portrayal) cognizant of her medical situation, without completely succumbing to the usual banalities: doctors and tears, the boundless fortitude of the patient, human solidarity, the purification of the mind through pain . . . No, thanks. Waiter: please take away these *Patch Adams* leftovers.

I'm going both with and against the grain of a lesson from Oscar Wilde: beauty is more important than existence. Beauty is real life.

In contrast to Wilde, who believed that real-life testimonies are inane, and that to transcend this inanity we must embellish our perception of the real by filling our surroundings with sublime objects, I find ornamentation (even the sublime runs the risk of becoming an ornament) a form of nouveauricheism, of obscenity. Transforming a collection of anecdotes into structure, on the other hand, offers the challenge of conquering a certain level of beauty: achieving a rhythm despite the soundproofed vulgarity that is life. Wilde thought writing autobiographically diminished the aesthetic experience. I don't agree: only the proximity and impurity of the two zones can produce meaning, and that is precisely what *The Ballad of Reading Gaol*—the only work signed with the immortal C.3.3.—is about. To formalize in syntax what happens to oneself (or rather, what one thinks happens) in the light of a neighboring body is (can become) something more than narcissism or psychotherapy: an art of the fugue. For this reason, *De Profundis* continues to be a beautiful, atypical, and difficult text. Of course, I'm not even the nail of Oscar Wilde's little finger. Yet I possess a very slight pragmatic advantage over him (in addition, naturally, to having relative freedom of movement, my forced labor is mental, and I use a computer; I'm a dandy): I do not "blame myself terribly" for not being able to write. Quite the contrary: even if the addict's love I feel for my mother were eventually to destroy my career (or anything else it might destroy), it will still be a love encoded in words. The hospital lechery that kidnaps and debases my energy and attention is, to some extent, sexually dead time. *Anima sola*. Time in which, in addition to a black hole, excellent working schedules come into being. My bankruptcy, my gaol, and my encyclical are one and the same impulse.

I write in order to transform the perceptible. I write to give voice to suffering. But I also write to make this hospital chair less uncomfortable and ordinary. To be a man capable of being inhabited (if only by ghosts) and, therefore, of being passed through: someone useful to Mamá. So long as I have the will, I can go out, negotiate friendships, ask for plain speech, buy things at the drugstore, and carefully count the change. So long as I can type, I can give form to what I don't know and, in that way, be more human. Because I write to return to her body: I write to return to the language that birthed me.

I want to learn to watch her die. Not here: in an ink-black

reflection: like Perseus glimpsing, on the surface of his mirror, the flection cutting off the head of Medusa.

And if Mamá doesn't die? Will so many sleepless hours at her bedside, the rigorous exercise of memory, not a little imagination, a certain grammatical decorum all be worth the effort? Will this Word file be worth the effort if my mother survives leukemia . . . ? Just asking that question makes me the worst of whores.

Mamá would be proud to know it, since she gave me my first, soundest lessons in style. She taught me, for instance, that a work of fiction is honest only when it maintains its logic in the materiality of discourse: Mamá, lying to the neighbors about her origins and profession with an exquisite vocabulary, impossible to compare with that of the other women in the barrio, impossible to imagine in the voice of a prostitute who completed only two years of elementary school. During my teenage years, she made me read Carreño's manual on urbanity and good manners and, immediately afterward, *The Executioner's Song*. In the latter, she'd underlined a passage describing a convict whose curious talent consisted of bending his neck and head forward over his torso with great agility to suck his own cock.

She permitted me the intuition that profound feelings don't allow for strict distinctions between sublime and banal foundations, and that the uneasy condition of beauty would be always cynically taken in usufruct by the dilettantes and bureaucrats of pleasure: it's easy to manipulate middle-class people with a smattering of learning by the use of a couple of famished iambs, but, in contrast, we are all ashamed of ignorance, that heartrending dark night of language. Once, when I was walking along the Coyuca Sand Bar near Acapulco, she squeezed my hand so tightly it was painful, and crooned commonplaces made popular by the then-fashionable singer Lorenzo Santamaría: so you never forget me, not even for a moment, and we live together in memories, so you never forget me. Then, crying, she stopped, knelt beside me, and said:

"You and I both know that song isn't going to get played on the radio forever."

A few weeks before Mamá fell ill, Heriberto Yépez wrote to me from Tijuana to tell me he'd met some of the famous L=A=N=G=U=A=G=E poets during a trip to Chicago and New York.

> The Language poets seem to me very intelligent, but 90 percent of the time they leave me cold. Meeting them in the flesh, I realized what was happening: they're typical intelligent gringos, but soulless. One day, Bruce Andrews, perhaps the most important of them, said, like he was asking for a glass of water, " I don't fuckin' care about spirituality." Hey, I want to go on believing he said that because he'd had three beers. I can't conceive of a poet without a spiritual vein. Without spirituality, there's no poetry.

I was on the verge of answering: of course. Because at that moment it seemed to me beyond question. But later, the leukemia came along, with its bottles of chemicals and its manual of demented exercises. Now I'm in the dark at my mother's bedside, it's night again, and the auditory blip of the hospital sometimes acts like a lie detector. Guadalupe "Charles" lies hooked up to the infusion pump of her sixth round of chemotherapy. Her blood pressure is low. Her gums are sore. She hasn't vomited, but she's been constipated for five days. The doctor prescribed Metamucil and lots of water, so Guadalupe's drinking six pints a day. She still isn't shitting, but she has to piss every twenty minutes. As she's hooked up to the black mask—my mother's nickname for the double entrance chemo catheter—I have to fetch the bedpan and place it under her buttocks, remove it when the sound stops, wipe her pussy with a Kleenex, and then pour the piss into the toilet bowl. A while ago, she wet the bed, and I had to call two ward auxiliaries to change the sheets. My antiseptic routine represents a more or less arduous task that—added to the coming and going of the doctors and nurses, the shift changes, the mealtimes, and the paying of bills and prescriptions—interrupts my writing. Could this be spirituality: being able to go from writing this sentence to undertaking my daily responsibilities without any silent space of perception intervening between the two? Could it be a profound horror of the void that makes me solicitous when it comes to cultivating excretions? If not, is it my blustering certainty that true redemption consists of (finally) looking the excrement in the eye just as I'm doing now: sitting comfortably in an armchair, without a god, without shoes? Is it a more subtle, mocking demon: this temptation or itch to repeat three times, à la Beetlejuice, without quite believing them, the words of Bruce Andrews: "I don't fuckin' care about spirituality / I don't fuckin' care . . ."?

And if Mamá gets better?

The day after tomorrow, they're going to hit her with the seventh round of chemicals. They're going to put more blood in and a new load of platelets. Then she'll be under observation for ten to fourteen days, which will include taking a new bone marrow sample (I can already hear the screams). And then maybe she'll be ready to go home.

When the possibility that she might recover occurs to me, my breathing becomes uneven; I stop being able to write with any ease. I have a *material* vision of what this is: a text. A structure. A structure, I should add, into which I've breathed a certain tragic air.

And if Mamá doesn't die? Will it be fair to you, *reader* (as nineteenth-century egomaniacs called this vein of anguish), if I lead you along false trails through a piece of writing with no daggers: a plasma discourse . . . ? Remember I'm a whore: I have a grant, the Mexican government pays me month after month to write a book. But just how can I progress with this task if the lyrical leukemia of my main character is brought to its knees by a science I lack . . . ?

This thing I write is a work of suspense. Not in its poetics; through its technique. Not for me, but for you.

Mamá Madrastra

Dear, sweet, good, human, social . . .
Eros Alesi

That at thirty-three, the age when Christ died, I formed a rock band and called it Madrastras, the Stepmothers. That—and I've never explained this before—I did so to mock my mother, the cadger, the tyrant, the abused sluttish daughter of a bitch I secretly called my stepmother because I was a princess and she was a meddlesome witch ruining my life—the best, the most ordinary—stealing a gold chain from my second wife, or telling me the correct way—her way—to change my first baby's diapers.

That she was always knocking at my door like God in a sonnet by Félix Lope de Vega y Carpio to remind me I'm half-caste trash, that all those diplomas and newspaper clippings singing my praises are nothing, that I sneaked into the middle class by the service entrance with holes in my sweater. That she'd call to me from the street. That I'd creep silently to my bedroom, close the door, snort one two eight lines of cocaine and she'd be down there shouting open up son and I know you're there I know you're in a real bad way I'm worried I'm sitting here without a cent to my name I haven't eaten all day I'm sick open up why are you like this why did you change into a mad dog and then another howl open up son please and another line for me.

That I said to myself: we'll open the door tomorrow, only to answer the same the next day.

That I stopped seeing her for years because her mere presence made me wretched. That a voice repeated in my head: it's her fault you're white trash. That she again mocked: but you're not white, you're a barefoot Indian a darkskin with a foreign name a biological joke a dirty mestizo and yes, yes: a piece of trash. That I prevented her from seeing my children so she wouldn't infect them. That for fear of infecting them (and because I'm not what they call a good person) I walked out on them. That I enjoyed life had orgasms more beautiful than an opium high. That I drank swallowed snorted smoked slept with ingenuous women sordid oral anal iconic drunken agile weak mental women true artists frigid passionate women companions in arms bastards of the House of Bourbon without ridding myself of this piercing in the limbo of my ear called two children contaminated by me. That I'm no longer a princess I'm a *papá padrastro* a stone in the shoe of their ruined adolescence.

That one night I told her she was fucking up my life. That she asked me for money. That she'd suffer days of depression about her lost beauty: slouched in an armchair wasting away at the expense of my risible salary in front of awful Mexican movies from the seventies on a freeview channel. That she blamed me for blaming her for everything. That she said if you're going to go just do it you great son of a whore but you're no longer my son for me you're just a mad dog. That I hated her from September 1992 to December 1999. That during those years I religiously set aside a moment for hating her every day with the same devotion others employ in saying the rosary. That I hated her again a few times in the following decade but unsystematically just out of habit: without a fixed timetable. That I've always loved her with the unbroken light of the morning she taught me to write my name.

That once when I was a kid someone attacked me in the street and Mamá took me to the police station to make a complaint but the blow hadn't left a trace. That to exaggerate the injury and ensure the perpetrator was punished she gave me a second kick on the ankle.

Mamá Leucemia

She phoned us early one Saturday. An exhibition of Mónica's artwork was about to open in Aguascalientes, so we were busy wrapping paintings and packing our bags.

She spoke to my wife for a while. Then to me. She mentioned her granddaughters, complained about the trucks passing by her door "making an infernal racket," criticized Paty Chapoy's Buddhism, praised Barack Obama . . . Her tone on the other end of the line was all wrong. She sounded like a little old woman.

"I need something," she said before hanging up. "I need you to buy me a walker. I'm so tired."

I said I would, and hung up.

Mónica thought it could be something serious.

"It's her way of blackmailing me for not having been to see her," I replied.

We stop by her house one night before taking to the road.

I don't like her house. The front is painted royal blue and has round windows with white frames. There are only about five feet between the roof and the turn in the stair leading to the second floor. Almost none of the electrical switches work: the lightbulbs are connected by frayed wires to sockets hidden behind a picture or an opening in the wall or a pile of old clothes, supposedly for sale. All the rooms are full of clutter: rickety chairs in eternal hope of repair; Frankenstein bedside tables assembled from pieces of other people's cast-off furniture found in the trash; magazines about medicine, or pseudoscientific enigmas from the nineties, with the damp stains of at least four rainy seasons; broken sewing machines; broken domestic appliances; fragments of Fisher-Price, Lili Ledy, and Mattel toys; schmaltzy phrases printed on shellac or colored and/or moldy acrylic; dishes, vases, pots, mainly plastic.

Opposite the front door are two large mirrors, a desk, a modern chrome chair, and a table covered in hairdressing equipment. This is La Estética: the business my mother and sister have been struggling to keep afloat for four years.

She doesn't come down to welcome us. Diana opens the door and escorts us up to Mamá's bedroom.

She is lying in bed with her eyes closed. The brown-paper tinge of her complexion seems diluted, sallow, as if covered by a layer of nixtamal. She tells us she's had a bad intestinal infection. That she couldn't work for four days, but lately has managed to go to the bathroom and is feeling better. Now, she says, she's just weak. She hasn't been eating properly. She promises to rectify that straightaway. She doesn't seem low.

Diana, who's been battling with Guadalupe's hypochondria for years, and has had enough of it, says sharply:

"You need to get out of bed."

Mónica and I look on in silence.

It's not as bad as all that, I think: she's only sixty-five. After fifteen or twenty minutes stroking her hair, I propose taking her to see the doctor. She says no. It's not necessary. She's fine now, and will be even better after my visit. She's being melodramatic, but not lying: she loves me. And I love her, although with that ambiguous passion of the Judas who flees from the story carrying with him, untouched, the small purse of silver coins . . .

(Is that why I'm relieved not to have to take her to the doctor? Is it a good son or a sociopath who, at that moment, walks with my bones . . . ?)

We head home and turn in early because the plan is to be away before dawn. I dream all night that I'm leaning over a toilet bowl, spitting out gobs of black saliva and trying to relieve my pain with a natural remedy, the label of which reads: *Hiel Ayudada*.

Days pass with no change in Mamá's condition. I phone Aldo Reyna, our family doctor, and ask him to visit her while I'm there. Aldo examines her with exasperating thoroughness. A look of alarm spreads across his face even before he's finished. He goes to the laboratory on the corner, asks for a kit, and, there and then, takes the necessary samples for a full blood and urine count.

"Why didn't you consult me earlier?" he reproaches me as we descend the staircase designed for a dwarf.

I don't know how to reply: I'm making sure he doesn't crack his head against the hobbit-height ceiling of the landing.

The results come back at about six. Aldo has had to attend a family dinner (it's National Doctors' Day), so Mónica goes to pick them up. Before talking to me, she rings him. Aldo asks her to read out two of the figures: leukocytes and platelets. There's a moment of confusion, anxiety, delay . . .

He then orders:

"Tell Julián we have to have her admitted immediately. Tell him to cancel any commitments for the next few weeks."

Falling ill possesses a daltonic perceptive range that spans from ruining your weekend to horror. The most acute station this train passes through is not to be found at the extremes but in some indefinite zone on its route: pain polished to the condition of a sacred diamond. Someone suddenly connects you up to a cable that intensifies everything. It's the sublime thunderclap of Kant deprived of lyrical frills and postprandial constitutionals; just damp cavern. A sensitive sphere. Except that spheres are a symbol of perfection. And to call what my mother is about to undergo perfection would be pure evil.

She was admitted to the ER and spent four hours in a long hall, punctuated by curtains, where someone is crying every two meters. They told me I could stay there, but should keep out of the way, so for a long time I ricocheted between nurses, doctors, desks, and oxygen tanks, listening to her scream, "What are you doing? Don't do that to me, please," and, "Twenty inches, twenty inches." After a while, Aldo came out from behind one of the curtains accompanied by another young doctor, whom he introduced as Valencia.

"She's not going anywhere," said Valencia. "Better get your head around the idea of a long stay. Drink plenty of water, eat bananas, have some comfortable clothes brought in. You're going to need blood donors. A lot of them. Your initial instinct will be to donate your own blood. Don't. How good are you at giving bad news?"

Outside the ER a small audience had already gathered: Mónica, Diana and Gerardo, Saíd and Norma. I joined them and we spent a few minutes smoking and drinking coffee while I brought them up to date. Then I completed all the necessary formalities and returned to the ER to look for Lupita. She'd gone: they had taken her to internal medicine. I spent almost two hours trying to find her.

In the meantime, the newly rechristened Guadalupe Charles was admitted into the male medical ward: there weren't any beds available in the female wing. As no family member was present, the nurses attempted to obtain the details needed for the register directly from her. Guadalupe responded to everything with “twenty inches, twenty inches,” the whites of her eyes showing and her head drooping to one side. They undressed her, put on a gown that left her butt uncovered. They sat her on a plastic wheelchair-cum-commode and pushed her to the toilet, which was occupied. As no family member was present, the nurses decided to leave her in the corridor for a while, with her ass there for all to see. When they finally showered her, they elected to do so without removing her from the wheelchair: using a long hooked pole, they slid the body under a stream of cold water, removed it, scrubbed it down, and then put it back under the shower for as long as they judged necessary to rinse off the soap.

When I managed to find her, she was in room 108 (the following day she was transferred to 101 to isolate her). She was lying next to an octogenarian emphysema sufferer, separated by nothing more than a transparent green curtain. Her hair was damp and spread on a towel. I touched her forehead and she half-opened her eyes. She murmured:

“We all have a space. I don’t know where, but I’ve got twenty inches to rest in. I’m so glad you brought them, my son.”

I began believing the earth was round when I started high school. My school was on the other side of the tracks, almost on the outskirts of the northern town we were then living in. By then we were poor enough to consider the daily public transportation costs beyond our means, so I had to walk some three miles every morning. The school bell rang at a disgusting hour: six forty-five. But at least I enjoyed the freedom of choosing between two routes for making the journey. I could take a half-mile detour to the south and cross the tracks separating my neighborhood from Federal No. 2, using the pedestrian bridge. Or I could sleep in for fifteen minutes longer and make the journey hanging between the carriages in the classification yard, with the additional adrenaline rush of leaping (wearing my backpack, like a parachutist in the U.S. Army) from trains moving deceptively fast.

It didn't take me long to celebrate the luck that, as a child, brought me into contact with Ferrocarriles Nacionales de México, a heap of scrap iron whose rolling stock and speeds had varied little since the time of the Revolution. The trains were like horses: lethal, raging wild animals, but at the same time fainthearted and lined up, tameable. Maneuvering between the wagons and watching the sun coming up on the other side was my way of getting out of Plato's cave. I understood it wasn't natural for a piece of steel to stand for a spike in my heart rate. Or at least that's what I imagine now, as the nurse sticks a needle into me and checks if I'm eligible to serve as a platelet donor.

One day I leapt from the moving coupling between two maize wagons and, when I came down on the other side and stumbled, simply knew it. What an idiot, I told myself. Why hadn't I seen it before? A sensation copied from Charlton Heston in *The Agony and the Ecstasy* when, while escaping from his father, Michelangelo goes into ecstasies at the sight of that miraculous Polaroid named Creation: a small cloud stretching out toward another small cloud. In that same meeting of surfaces, floating like a silk or gauze *anime* from the moving train to the crystal-wind boundary of open space, feeling happily out of focus, I perceived it with Saiyanian lucidity:

The earth is a sphere.

Obviously.

I don't have much experience of death. I guess this could eventually become a logistical problem. I should have rehearsed with some junkie friend or grandmother with heart problems. But no. I'm sorry, there's been a gap in my education. If it happens, I'll make my debut in the major league: burying Mamá.

One day I was playing guitar at home when someone came to the gate. It was a neighbor. She was sobbing.

"Would you mind not playing your guitar? Cuquín was knocked down by a Coca-Cola truck. It killed him. We're holding the vigil right now."

I was fifteen and loud.

I extended them the courtesy of keeping quiet. Instead of playing, I got my Walkman and put on *Born in the U.S.A.*

After a while they came back and rang more insistently. It was my namesake, the neighbor's son, brother of the dead boy. He said:

"Come with me to buy some ice."

I put on a shirt—it was summer: in the 116-degree heat of the Coahuila desert, you don't wear much indoors—jumped over the railing, and walked to the beer store with him.

He explained:

"He's beginning to smell. But Mom and Dad are trying to ignore it."

We bought four bags of ice. On our way back, my namesake

stopped on the corner and began to cry. I hugged him. We stood there like that for a while. Then we lifted the bags from the ground and I went to his house with him. Wails and cries were coming from inside. I helped him take the bags onto the porch, said good-bye, and returned to my headphones.

That episode is on my mind now because something similar happened the other night. I went out to buy water in the OXXO store opposite the hospital. On my way back, I noticed a pedestrian making hard work of weaving through the traffic on the avenue. At some point, just before getting to where I was, he stopped between two cars. Horns were very soon honking. I deposited my bottles of water, went up to him, and tugged him back to the sidewalk. As soon as he felt my hand, he slid both arms around my chest and began to cry. He was murmuring something about his "little one"; I wasn't sure if he was referring to his daughter or his wife. He asked if I could let him have a telephone card, and I gave him mine. There's something repulsive in the embrace of a person crying for a loss of life: they grab hold of you like you're a slab of meat.

I know nothing about death. I only know about mortification.

In the last year of my adolescence, when I was sixteen, there was a second corpse in my neighborhood. And neither then did I have the courage to view the coffin, because I feel—and this hasn't changed—I formed part of the unforeseeable chain of circumstances leading to the death. He was called David Durand Ramírez and was younger than me. He died one September day in 1987, at eight in the morning, from a shot fired from a .22-caliber pistol. This tragedy was partly the reason for my family migrating to Saltillo, my decision to study literature, my choice of career, and, eventually, the fact that I was sitting in the leukemia ward narrating my mother's story. But to explain how David Durand's death marked my life, I have to begin earlier: several years before.

This all happened in Ciudad Frontera, a town of some thirty thousand inhabitants that had sprung up in the shadow of the steelworks in Monclova, Coahuila State, where my family experienced its most comfortable years, but also a catalog of humiliations.

We'd arrived there after the closure of the brothels in Lázaro Cárdenas. Mamá went in search of sympathetic magic: she thought in that other city where a steel foundry was also under construction, our household would again experience the bonanza of the Lázaro Cárdenas years.

In the beginning, she wasn't wrong: in a brothel called Los Magueyes, she met Don Ernesto, an elderly local cattle rancher. He started frequenting her as just one more whore, but as the months passed, he began to realize my mother was no fool: she read a lot, had a rare talent for arithmetic, and—crazy as this may sound—was a woman of very firm principles. She was, above all, incorruptible when it came to other people's money, something that, in this country, almost makes you a foreigner.

Don Ernesto took her on as his eyes and ears in a couple of businesses: another brothel and the town's gas station. He offered her a fair wage and affectionate treatment. None of which stopped him turning up from time to time, having had one tequila too many, and putting his hand under her skirt, a maneuver she had to dodge without losing her job or her composure.

Marisela Acosta was happy. She organized her children to look after one another so as not to squander more money on neurotic childminders. She rented a house with three bedrooms and a small yard; acquired some furniture and a dilapidated sky-blue Ford. She brought humus-rich soil from Lamadrid and planted a small plot of carrots that never grew. The name of our neighborhood was ominous: El Alacrán, the scorpion. But however schmaltzy it may sound (and will sound: What else can you expect from a story that takes place in the Sweet Nation?), we lived on the corner of Progreso and Renacimiento, at number

537. There, from 1980 to 1982, between progress and renaissance, we spent our infancy: my mother's and mine.

Then came the massive devaluation of the peso, known as the "Dog Crisis"—after the president had promised he would defend the currency like a dog—and, in my childhood pantheon, José López Portillo entered posterity as (in my mother's words) the Great Son of a Bitch. Don Ernesto's out-of-town businesses went bankrupt. He returned to his cattle and sacked Marisela. We held on to the house, but began making seasonal migrations again: Acapulco, Oaxaca, Sabinas, Laredo, Victoria, Miguel Alemán . . . Mamá attempted, for the umpteenth time, to earn a living as a sewing machine operator in the Teycon bonded assembly plant in Monterrey. The pay was so low it was criminal, and she was hired at piece rate, two or three shifts a week. She always ended up going back to the daytime brothels on Calle Villagrán, squalid dives crammed by midmorning with soldiers and cops more interested in the clothes than the women, which added a tinge of violence and wretchedness to the air.

It was soon impossible to keep up with the rent for the house. At the end of '83 we were evicted, and all our possessions seized. Almost all of them: at my express request, the clerk of court allowed me to remove a book or two before the police loaded our things onto the van. I took the two thickest: the complete works of Wilde in an Aguilar edition, and volume 13 of the *Nueva Enciclopedia Temática*. Literature has always been generous with me: if I had to go back to that moment, knowing what I know now, I'd choose the same books.

We spent three years in absolute poverty. Mamá had acquired a plot on disputed common land, but there was nothing there besides dwarf sand dunes, dead cacti, half a truckload of gravel, three hundred blocks, and two sacks of cement. We erected a small room with no foundations that came more or less as high as my shoulders, and added a roof of cardboard sheets. To get in, you had to go on all fours. There was no running water, no drains, no electricity. Jorge left high school and found a job mixing nixtamal in the tortilla section of an industrial canteen. Saíd and I sang on buses for money. Mamá—who by then had given birth to Diana, my little sister—was always away on trips.

Within a year, Jorge had had enough: he grabbed some clothes and left. He was seventeen. We next received news of him on his twenty-third birthday: he'd just been appointed duty manager at the Hotel Vidafel in Puerta Vallarta. He added in his letter that it was a seasonal post.

"I was born in Mexico by mistake," he once told me. "But one of these days I'm going to put that right once and for all."

And he did: at the age of thirty, he emigrated to Japan.

I can't talk about my mother or myself without referring to this period. Not for its sad, pathetic aspects, but because it's our version of spirituality: a hybrid between Buñuel's *The Young and the Damned* and *The Dhammapada*. Or better still, and less run-of-the-mill: Pedro Infante's *Nosotros los Pobres* in mystic karate master costumes; *The 36th Chamber of Shaolin*. Three years of dire poverty don't destroy you. Just the reverse: they awaken a certain visceral lucidity.

Singing on the interurban buses that transported the staff of the AHMSA foundry back to the dry archipelago of neighboring towns (San Buenaventura, Nadadores, Cuatro Ciénegas, Sacramento, Lamadrid), Saíd and I saw almost crystalline sand dunes, black-and-white hills, deep walnut groves, a river called Cariño, pools of fossil water with stromatoliths, giraffe-necked box turtles . . . We had our own money and ate whatever took our fancy. The refrain we finished all our performances with went: "I do what I do / 'cause I don't wanna steal." We learned to think like artists: we sold a stretch of the landscape.

At times, our Coahuiltec version of the Arabian simoon would blow in. It was a strong wind that used to take off the sheets of cardboard covering the shack. When that happened, Saíd and I would go running after our roof, which would be twisting, turning, and flying low down the middle of the street.

From 1986 (the year the World Cup was held in Mexico) to 1987 (the year David Durand died), things got quite a lot better: we rented a house, bought some furniture, and gradually rejoined the class of the "poor but respectable." Except that Marisela Acosta, unbeknownst to most of the neighborhood, had to go four nights a week to the brothels of the nearby city of Monterrey to earn the money for our schooling.

I was in the first year of high school and, despite the stigma of having been a beggar in the eyes of half the town, had slowly managed to renew my friendship with the Durands, a fair-haired family of French descent that had little money (the father was a truck driver) but were very popular.

One night, Gonzalo Durand asked me to go to La Acequia with him. He wanted to buy a pistol.

Gonzalo was a sort of alpha male for us members of the street-corner gang who met up in the evenings to smoke marijuana and flirt with the girls coming out of the high school. Not only was he the oldest: he was also the best fighter and the only one of us with a good job, an operator in the no. 5 hot metal furnace at AHMSA. He was just nineteen. The age of armed illusions.

The elite chosen to accompany him on his rite of passage were Adrián Contreras and me. We made our way in an unregistered '74 Maverick to the adjoining neighborhood. First they offered him a Smith & Wesson revolver ("It's a Bone Collector," said the assistant in a syrupy voice, most probably pumped to the ass with cough mixture). Then they showed him the small automatic pistol. He fell in love with it straight off and bought it.

The next day Adrián Contreras came around and said:

"Something terrible's happened. Gonzalo accidentally fired off a shot and killed El Güerillo in his sleep."

The first image that came into my head was ominous: Gonzalo, sleepwalking, peppering his family with bullets . . . But no: he'd come off the night shift and, wide-awake and impatient, gone straight home, climbed up into his bunk, and begun to clean the pistol under the sheets. A bullet had somehow gotten into the chamber. Gonzalo, who knew nothing about firearms, hadn't even realized. At some point, the pistol slipped from his hands. Trying to grab it, he accidently pulled the trigger. The projectile went through the bunk and hit his little brother, sleeping below him, in the belly.

David Durand was, what . . . ? Fourteen years old? He'd once run away with his girlfriend. Presumably, he wanted to get married. Their parents gave them each a good thrashing. He died in Gonzalo's arms, on the seat of the Maverick, on the way to the hospital.

Adrián and I turned up at the burial service, but didn't dare go into the chapel. We were afraid any moment someone would ask, "But where did that bastard get hold of a pistol . . . ?"

Gonzalo was in prison for a couple of months. That was the last I heard of him. Mamá, very serious, said:

"You'll regret it if I ever see you looking at firearms or hanging around with those blots on the landscape again."

The rest of the year passed. One day, just before Christmas, Mamá came home very early, still smelling of alcohol. Saíd, Diana, and I used to sleep huddled up together in the same bed to keep warm. Mamá switched on the light, sat down beside us, and sprinkled our heads with a shower of wrinkled bills. Her makeup was like a clown's and there was a small red wound visible on her forehead.

She said:

"Let's go."

And just like that, without packing or stripping the house down, we fled from the hometown of my childhood.

Every so often, I go back to Monclova to give a lecture or as part of a book tour. Sometimes we drive around the edge of Ciudad Frontera, on our way to the pools in Cuatro Ciénegas, or to gather pomegranates in Mabel and Mario's farm in Lamadrid. I say to Mónica, as we drive along the Carlos Salinas de Gortari bypass, "I lived behind that airport when I was a kid." She replies, "Let's go there." And I say no.

One day she wakes up slagging off the nurses.

"They're scumbags, Julián. I spend twenty hours hooked up to the black mask. They switch off the pump, and I tell them I want a shower, and one of them says, 'Go on then. Get on with it. I'll bring you a clean gown in a minute.' Can you believe it? And me with the needle skewered in my arm and the IV tubing still hanging from the stand, dragging the empty bag of my chemotherapy around like a lost soul. Can you believe it? And there's no way I can say, 'Just how, you moron, am I supposed to take off the gown if you don't disconnect me from that bag of trash first?' Because these ladies here get in a huff if they so much as hear you breathe. They're scumbags."

My sister leaves the room and says to the girl on duty:

"She's beginning to love you like a daughter."

I guess all this could be interpreted as good news. But the temptation to hope is the most dangerous of all. Letting your guard down. Not my style. If she recovers, maybe. If she dies, no way. There's no blessing comparable to the act of loving your mother, watching her grow weaker and doing absolutely nothing. I mean, nothing emotional: signing checks, going to meetings with doctors, drumming up blood donations. Nothing more.

This month, my life is more like a political campaign than a tragedy. I listen for my cell phone the whole day. Shake hands. Hug people. I give the nurses books and candy. I treat my wife and sister as if they were my media coordinators, the doctors like backers, the officials like my party leaders, my acquaintances like a moronic, easily influenced bunch of voters . . . I treat my mother's weakened body as if it were a piece of proposed legislation. Look at her: she's broken, she's running a fever, she needs your blood, she was never up to much, but with a little help from you, with our confidence, with the help of the youth, she'll soon be something more than a pain or an invention of mine getting covered in sores in a narrow bed. Soon she'll be cured and will be a symbol of the Triumph of Good at the Heart of Our Society.

Good days.

Bad days.

For example, Friday: they allowed her a break from the chemo, but instead of resting she made everyone around her suffer. She got out of bed, showered without help, asked for the meager hair she had (the chemo had been leaving her balder by the day) to be cut, ate heartily and sat in the chair, requested a Jennifer Aniston chick flick, and went on the whole time about how she was ready to go home. The next morning there was a power outage in the hospital and we were eight hours late in transfusing the platelet apheresis. Her anemic complexion returned, and she scarcely had the energy to arch her back when we brought the bedpan. In a whisper, clenching her jaws, she said to me:

"Please, take me out of here. Take me home. I don't want to die looking at this ridiculous colored flooring."

Good days.

Bad days.

Thanks to the leukemia, I came to understand that provisionality is not a choice: it's the stark rhythm of the mind. It's hardly been three weeks, but human contact, as I've known it, has vanished, swallowed by the microscopic tsunami of cancer. Human contact has become a sticky substance. An archipelago of clots, packaged and refrigerated under the oily light of the blood bank. She's a vampire and I'm her Renfield: Mamá had drunk from the veins of half my friends.

First they requested five units of red blood cells. They already had B positive, so it didn't matter which blood group we deposited in exchange. Over twenty donors turned up. Almost all of them women. Only three candidates passed the test: all the girls were anemic, and the majority of the males were promiscuous, took drugs, or had gotten tattoos in the preceding months. Then they asked for more: four, five, six, seven bags. They are like livers embalmed by Mattel. One Tuesday, around eighteen of us got together to collect the rest of the transfusions Lupita needed. The Grand Intellectual Marathon for a Good Cause: join up, help, participate.

One by one, we went in.

The blood bank has an Aztec altar blade. Those who have been rejected come out with tears in their eyes, ashamed, folding the piece of paper with diagrams explaining why their blood isn't right for the sacrifice. Periodic poets. Malnourished singers. Painters with thin veins. Historians with an excess of red cells. Virus-laden journalists. Culture professionals without platelets. A whole altarpiece of champions of civilization made ridiculous by a frigging needle.

So far, the mortification had been more or less Rabelaisian, although governed by Darwinian and fiduciary logic: I need your blood, give it to me in exchange for that mercantile zone of idealism we term Friendship. Something reducible, if only metaphorically, to the IMF. But later they requested the first of twelve platelet aphereses. The platelets are in a thick liquid vaguely resembling pineapple juice. To extract them, the torture victim has to be connected to a machine that extracts his blood, sucks out the yellow soul, and returns the red chaff to the hostage body. When I say "torture victim," I'm not using the term figuratively: ask someone who has donated platelets how it feels. Talk about luxury: extracting two pints of apheresis costs the same as three bottles of your average Moët & Chandon. Mamá sybaritic and Gothic.

My uncle Juan—my great-uncle, in fact—was a witch hunter. Mamá says he hunted them with a length of blessed cord, a rosary, a white sheet, a red candle made from animal fat, and the sharp edge of a bottle top, his fingers forming a cross, scoring the back of the Evil One twenty times.

"Witches have to be caught using two methods," Marisela would explain, grazing our goose-pimpled arms with her long nails during certain nights of the happy period when we lived in the Alacrán neighborhood. "With prayers and dirty tricks. Because mention of God makes them angry, and vulgarity mixed with holy artifices catches them on the hop. Your uncle Juan was an old hand, a master of capture. First he'd bombard them with Our Fathers, then he'd call them sluts and daughters of bastard fathers. He used to prowl around their cabins (because in olden days witches lived in the countryside; they didn't like cities) and alternate prayers and obscenities while fingering his rosary beads or knotting the Holy Cord. Sometimes he sang songs to seduce them. The Cuban songs he and grandfather Pedro used to like: 'On the Trunk of a Tree, a Child' or 'Sleep Peacefully beneath the Ground.' Sometimes he even played the guitar. And then he'd start again: Go fuck your mother, you frigging witch. Holy Mary, mother of God, pray for us sinners. It drove them crazy. And on and on until the devilish woman would come out of her cabin and fly into the nearest tree in the form of an owl."

Mamá never believed those stories. She related them because they were part of our inheritance, and because we used to beg to hear them.

At first, she'd say no.

"You're not dumb enough to believe superstitions, but not serious enough to deal with them. You'll have nightmares till dawn, and then it's me who doesn't sleep."

(This last remark was particularly directed at me; I was chickenhearted as a child.)

In the end, we'd manage to persuade her.

She had an extraordinary talent for oral narrative. To give her story fluidity, she'd walk around the kitchen table, preparing something or other: doughnuts, coffee with rich brown sugar, maize tortilla dessert. She'd gather up her hair (which she'd begun to wear shorter: barely past her shoulders) and, looking the other way, stroke the backs of our necks to give us a fright.

"'With this cord, I tie you to the earth,' Juan would repeat seven times, the number of white magic. He'd repeat those words over and over, tying knots in the Sacred Cord as he walked around the tree chosen by the witch. The owl (and you should be aware there's no such thing as a good owl: they're all quick-change artists or members of some troupe of damned souls) would retreat further into the tree, wanting to fly but unable to do so: even though it's in the tree, the knots of the blessed cord are binding its wings to the earth. Then, when the owl was already pretty stunned, my uncle Juan would lasso it and wrap it in a white sheet. He'd cover it in scratches by making the sign of the cross on its body with a sharp bottle top, while repeating and calling out foul words and prayers. And, finally, he'd scorch its wings with the molten wax of the red candle."

(I wonder if the Society for the Protection of Animals existed in that near-legendary era.)

Mamá used to finish the story in different ways. In some versions, the witch escaped, leaving Uncle Juan with the scar "he carries on his face to this day, as proof of that fierce battle." In others, the owl was reduced to ashes: shuddering and uttering dreadful insults, its body was consumed by the fire. Then there were two, maybe three, evil beasts. Or one very beautiful beast, whose sins Uncle Juan managed to redeem after falling in love with her long hair.

"And where does Uncle Juan live, Ma? Why doesn't he ever visit us?"

Mamá would turn down the heat a little under one of her stews.

"Uncle Juan plays guitar in the cantinas in Laredo. And we don't need him to come and see us. We're not part of that filthy world any longer."

"What are you dreaming about, my love?" asks Mónica.

I'm laughing in my sleep. Without waking, I say:

"I know how to put the chalk on the doors."

It's a happy dream. Mónica knows it: I never learned how to draw.

After a while the image drifts: the wall I'm drawing on belongs to a sanatorium. I'm wearing a gown, I'm hospitalized, my butt uncovered. The nurses pamper me, they come to say hello to me one by one. You can see they think I'm handsome. They lay me down on the shady side. Next to my mattress there's a window. Someone says:

"Don't open it, lad, never open it. A vampire owl lives in that tree over there."

Smiling, I agree. They're crazy, they like me. People in this fucking country are so ignorant.

After a while I prepare a syringe. I'm going to give Mamá an injection for her fever. I know how to do it. I'm her doctor. In my dream, she's lying on a hospital bed, identical to the hospital bed where she actually sleeps. I've told her I'm going to cure her. I ask for swabs, measure out the dose. A solicitous man with a mustache and gray hair, wearing a blue gown, asks if he can help me. He looks like Humberto, the head nurse on the evening shift in male medical at the U.H. I say no, turn my back on him. And suddenly I remember: shit, dammit, I'd opened the window. It's the son of the frigging vampire owl that lives in the tree. I turn and see him in the bed, in Mamá. *In*, not beside. Not fucking her either. *In*: halfway inside her, as if they were twins, or as if one of them was a glove puppet. I grab its hand. I tug. I say, "Go fuck your mother, you frigging witch." But the vampire owl doesn't come out from between the sheets. It just smiles. Without evil intent. A stupid smile.

I know that to beat it I have to pray like my great-uncle did.

I can't.

I can sing to it, tie it up, seduce it, say foul words to it, score its cheeks with a bottle top. Pray, no. Not praying is all I have.

II

HOTEL MANDALA

THE LEGO GIRAFFE

I am simply a self-conscious nerve in pain.

Oscar Wilde

1

When I write "here" again, it's summer and the sun is coming up. I've spent the last ten days on the eighth floor of a five-star hotel. The Mandala, Potsdamerplatz, Berlin. I'm typing on a laptop, doing a balancing act on my bloated belly, and, hidden among the faux-Zen luxury of a bathroom decorated in minimalist metal and etiolated flowers, I'm sweating out the sweet stink of a hangover. Dark wheat beer. Less than a block away, ninety feet below, screened in graffiti, lies the melodramatic rubble of my generation: a wall whose multicolored layers seem, rather than a postmodern relic, the slobbery remnants of a jawbreaker history couldn't chew. Like me: I can't sleep. I find the European summer sky—all smooth whiteness after four in the morning—disconcerting. From the window, I can see the neon frills framing the denuded cubicles of the DB Building, cool architecture that hypnotizes me with its undertones of disquiet: every night, in the mercury vapor illumination, I dream my mother is a cadaver lying on the asphalt in front of a hospital of light. Mónica is sleeping in the bedroom, a few steps away from me. Her belly, six months into pregnancy, swells from under her pajama top. I'm waiting for her to wake up before packing our bag to return—with neither a job nor money—home.

This is the second time I've visited Germany. The first was

three years ago. Mónica and I had been living together for a few months when I received an invitation to a poetry festival. It involved stopovers in Munich, Berlin, and Bonn. My first impulse was to make an excuse, because I'd never traveled outside Mexico and was thinking (maybe as an ingenuous form of revenge directed at my elder brother) of not altering that situation. Mónica must have persuaded me to get a passport; my first. She then made plane reservations, drew up a budget, negotiated our lodging, and it was all done and dusted: we set out on our honeymoon to the cold.

In the weeks leading up to the trip, I had a recurring dream. I was finally visiting Europe, the magical land all my friends celebrated with gusto, waving sacred photo albums before my shortsighted eyes. Unlike everyone else, I never managed to see a damned thing. The buildings seemed too tall and hermetic, the sidewalks very narrow, the streets tortuous. It was like taking a walk through a cemetery of Führers, each one interred in a bunker of his choice. The nightmare came to me almost daily while we were making our preparations, then in waiting rooms, customs areas, during the tedious transfers . . . A repugnant sensation that became more acute when we disembarked, in the middle of a freezing autumn, in Tegel airport: visually unappealing, crammed with passengers, narrow and functional, as if it had been constructed by a government housing agency. I had the feeling that, rather than arriving in another country, I was entering a really well-maintained, clean Mexican bus terminal, the sort I was perpetually visiting, hand in hand with Marisela Acosta, in the seventies.

In the arrivals hall, we were met by Anne, a very kind, anxious girl who first apologized for transporting us by bus rather than in a taxi. The festival's financial resources were minimal, she explained. She offered two options for the journey: going directly to the hotel by the shortest route—to the east—or taking a half-hour detour to the area around Charlottenburg, with a transfer to the U-Bahn, so as to get a glimpse of the center of old West Berlin, and pass by the Tiergarten. We didn't understand much: ignorance and jet lag are powerful narcotics. Mónica opted for the second proposal, thinking less of ourselves than of our host's enthusiasm. Anne wanted to help us with our suitcase; she seemed so tiny and defenseless, we wouldn't let her. We boarded an ultramodern bus—its panoramic windows, however, couldn't help but remind me of the Mexico City trolley buses I used to take in the eighties—and headed off on a tour from the northwest heading south, tracing a perpendicular line to Straße des 17 Juni. In her charmingly stiff Spanish, Anne provided a running commentary of what was passing outside: "That's a famous building, I think, that I don't know what it's called, but they're deconstructing because the ceiling has asbestos"; "Here we will see the Technological University"; "Now we're going to pass far off by part of the monument that is the Gold Elsa . . ." Another mirage: I believed I caught a distant glimpse, from a trolley bus, of the Angel of Independence on Mexico City's Avenida Reforma. Only in this case the sculpture was really majestic, more golden than ever, and framed by a forest, as if I'd regressed to being a teenager in a parallel world, and the mayor of the capital had ordered the clouds to be washed and streets closed to traffic to celebrate the fact that Mexico was finally the champion of its own soccer World Cup . . .

We transferred from the bus to the U-Bahn and hummed along to Friedrichstraße station. From there we continued on foot to our hotel, the Baxpax, scarcely a block from Oranienburger Straße.

Quite suddenly, as if with a single gulp I'd melted all the ice of my hallucinations, I felt completely relaxed. The Mitte turned out to be not only more habitable than Tegel, or the west of the city, but even welcoming. There was a whiff of the Condesa neighborhood in the air, with added hints of curry and Pakistan. But also, sheltering in certain venerable doorways, were beautiful Hungarian and Russian prostitutes with long, high-heeled boots and ultratight corsets gracefully tied, not over their skin, but over goose-down jackets. This trick allowed them to preserve, and even exaggerate, the desirability of their figures without succumbing to the thirty-five-degree wind. I could still sense the heavy lethargy of an inhuman architecture, as if the mental aroma of the Famous Wall was enveloping each new brick in its mixture of blackmail and bridal veil. But I found myself suddenly fond of the narrow, cramped streets of the old Jewish quarter. I don't know: perhaps the ghosts of prudish, pre-Nazi, socialist whoring have a family resemblance to my own tutelary phantoms.

Mónica and I did practically nothing the whole time we were in Germany. In Munich, we ate Italian olives and took hundreds of photos of a set of miniature gargoyles, specially designed to relieve the boredom of disoriented tourists. In Bonn, we went to look at the Rhine: a bit of an anticlimax with its Rhenish joggers of varying degrees of obesity grumbling about our slow pace. We occasionally had breakfast with other Latin American poets, who seemed deeply self-satisfied with their own genius. Or we chatted with Timo and Rike, our hosts. We always spoke in Spanish, utilizing a secret formula of idiomatic phrases and accents that, as soon as it emerged from Wilson Bueno's Paraguayan sea, fell headlong in a long-winded, hip-hop flood. It was a language that had been fleetingly imperial, before dragging itself along through the proud sewers and junkyards of junkie-filled, overpopulated cities, violent national anthems intoned by squat, swaggering countries that lose almost every one of their wars; nations and subnations and regurgitations whose only Bolivarian dream is called Nike, is called Brangelina, is called for-the-love-of-god-will-someone-pull-the-four-hairs-from-Chavez's-nose . . . The best poets were, naturally, from Cuba and Chile. But when it came to conversation, nothing doing: they would have had to send them over with built-in subtitles.

What Mónica and I preferred (I'm not sure we enjoyed it: rather, we suffered it with incoherent lyrical depth) was walking along the empty, autumnal Berlin streets. We made a point of veering off between three-story apartment buildings whose central courtyards, dedicated to trade, seemed like the Odradek or golem of a mall by the sea. Or we would shelter from the evening's howling gale in exquisite Turkish cafés, in the doorways of which a boy would be selling hashish and sprigs of lavender. Or we went deep into the area around the Volkspark Friedrichshain, walking along streets that unfailingly led to small squares, each with its inevitable gray church with green and gold ornamentation, and a crush barrier around a public work of art and—right here, or over there—an unfortunate equestrian statue, romantically impeccable in its isolation. None of those images were either flattering or sad. It was, instead, like entering an interior landscape on tiptoe.

There's a Ray Bradbury story in which two hobos earn a living by taking over a lookout point by the highway: they charge anyone who pulls over two dollars to get an advance view of the city. The success of the ragged entrepreneurs is due to the fact that, by some miraculous ruse, each driver views from the hillside the city that is the object of his most burning desire: some see New York; others Paris; a young student describes what he sees by reciting from memory Coleridge's *Kubla Khan* . . . If I could pay two dollars to stand on that lookout point, Berlin below zero would be my bombed Xanadu.

In an effort to compensate for our cultural ineptitude, each morning we set out to visit a museum. We almost never followed through with this plan: there was always a shop selling knickknacks or some street stall to divert us from our mission. In Hackescher Markt, along Hackescherhöfe, going up Rosenthalerplatz and beyond, Invalidenstraße and Kastanienallee and the Prenzlauerberg neighborhood, our route was not dictated by historical prestige, but by the omnipotent junk: Chinese plastic beads, vintage pin-ups with inscriptions in Swedish, a polymer ring in the form of a stylized panther, an absinthe boutique, fake relics of the GDR, hundreds of late nineteenth- and early twentieth-century tapestries, reproduced without copyright on wrapping paper, lighters and pens and small bottles of oil and CDs of eighties Italian ballads and tin dolls with moving pieces and aluminum necklaces coated with powdered dye and little books with pictures of the Fernsehturm highlighted with silver ink: mass-produced trash, identical in spirit to the plastic frogs sold on the stalls opposite the Zócalo in Mexico City. Serve us another round of Taiwan.

But when we happened to detach ourselves from the sidewalk treasures and enter some distinguished locale housing the Germanic patrimony (the Bode, the Pergamon, Friedrich Wilhelm III's apartments), the experience turned out to be heartrendingly unremarkable: tall Roman jars for serving wine, Greek vessels decorated with images of gigantic pricks, marble heads battered to a greater or lesser extent by sticks and swords, Phoenician coins, tiny Cretan dolls whose size and orifices seemed perfect for making key chains . . . Hardware, no less tacky for being ancient. The difference isn't in the object itself but in the story behind it. A solid gold fish encrusted with precious stones that a fisherman's net trawled from the bottom of the Spree: the piece is so sumptuous it seems akin to Mexican narco jewelry. The bust of an Egyptian lady with unplucked eyebrows. A Hellenic frontispiece that, after being thrown in the garbage, became a marble Lego model with pieces gone, never to return . . .

When the night drew in, we'd return to the hotel and, freezing cold, make love. We'd talk for a while in the dark, looking out through the mist at the illuminated cupola of the Oranienburger Straße. Then Mónica would slowly fall asleep. I'd cover her up, get dressed, grab my Walkman, and go out in search of a drink on the icy streets of Spandau. Sometimes I'd stop to talk—in mutually incomprehensible English—with transvestites and prostitutes. Sometimes I'd buy a bottle of 136-proof Moulin Vert absinthe and, stashing it under my overcoat, go up into the S-Bahn. All alone, with no destination in mind. I'd drink until the shadow of the bare lime trees and the velocity of the street-lit public became blots: black and white ink transecting the print of Berlin like a cup of tea spilled on the plans of a sacred city.

2

As a child I was called Favio Julián Herbert Chávez. Now, in the civil registry in Chilpancingo, they say that was not in fact the case. The copy of the birth certificate differs from the original in one letter: it says "Flavio." I don't know if this was out of spite on the part of my parents or a mistake made by the previous or present bureaucracy. Under the name of "Flavio," I had to renew my passport and my electoral ID. So all my childhood memories come, inevitably, with an error. The name I use for the simplest of acts (holding a spoon, reading this line) is different from the one I use to cross borders or vote for the president of my country. My memory is a notice written by hand on cardboard, posted outside an airport equipped with Prodigy Mobile, a brokerage house, and a Sanborns department store: "Welcome to Mexico."

I was born on January 20, 1971, in the port city of Acapulco de Juárez, Guerrero State. At the age of three, I saw my first dead body: a drowned man. And also my first guerrilla: Kito, the younger brother of my godmother, Jesu: he was doing time for a bank heist. I spent my childhood traveling from city to city, whorehouse to whorehouse, following the itinerancy imposed on the family by my mother's profession. Year after year, I journeyed from the far south, armed with fierce patience, to the splendid cities of the north.

I thought I'd never leave the country. I thought I'd never get out of poverty. I've worked—I say this without meaning to offend, paraphrasing an illustrious statesman, an exemplar of the sublime national idiosyncrasy—doing things *not even the blacks* are prepared to do. I've had seven long-term relationships—Aída, Sonia, Patricia, Ana, Sol, Anabel, Lauréline, and Mónica—and very few casual lovers. I have fathered two sons: Jorge, who is now seventeen, and Arturo, fifteen. I was a cocaine addict during some of the happiest and most dreadful periods of my life. I once helped remove a dead body from the highway. I smoked crystal meth off a lightbulb. I went on a fifteen-day triumphal tour as the lead singer in a rock band. I went to university and studied literature. I lost an academic progress competition whose prize was to meet the president. I'm left-handed. None of those things prepared me for my mother's leukemia. None of those things made the forty days and nights I spent sitting sleepless at her bedside less squalid. Noah plowing his way through a flood of blood chemicals, caring for and hating her, watching her fever rise to the point of asphyxiation, noting her encroaching baldness. I'm a brute who, with my head spinning, travels north from the southern ruins of an ancient civilization toward a Second Coming of the Barbarians: bon voyage; Free Market; USA; the death of your fucking mother.

A few weeks before coming to Berlin, I had to spend hours in the Ministry of Foreign Affairs. It wasn't for myself: Sonia, the mother of my son Arturo, is moving to Texas. Arturo still hasn't decided whether to go with her or stay on a year with his grandparents before enrolling in a gringo high school. In either case, he needs to renew his passport. He can't: he's a minor, I'm his father, and he needs my authorization. And I can't give it: according to the Mexican civil registry, I no longer exist. My name is no longer my name. *Je est un autre*, and unlike Rimbaud, I have documents to prove it.

Arturo, Sonia, and I had arranged to meet very early outside the ministry. It took us until midday to complete all the red tape. Then, when they were about to add the much-prized stamp with the national coat of arms, the young woman noticed a minute typographical discrepancy between my passport and my son's birth certificate. She became very serious.

"But just look at us," I tried joking. "We're like two peas in a pod."

The young woman didn't deign to reply. Turning to my wife, she said:

"There's a discrepancy. I'll have to consult my superiors."

Making a face, Sonia ordered me (as if I too were her child, a strange idea I've been unable to rid myself of since the day we married) to go out into the street with Arturo and let her sort things out.

Sitting on a bench opposite the ministry, Arturo picked up the thread of our conversation.

"Then he sent a letter saying he'd killed another woman, one nobody thought he'd murdered. But a long time had gone by. And that's how they knew he wasn't in fact dead, and if it hadn't been for the DNA, and a computer file, and a security camera in a Home Depot, he'd never have been caught."

He was talking about the BTK strangler. Lately, Arturo has been giving me detailed accounts of the lives of famous murderers whenever we see each other. An Argentinian boy with big ears who committed five or six homicides before reaching puberty. A vindictive guru who threw poison gas into the Japanese metro. The famous Goyo Cárdenas, honored by Congress . . . Not long ago he discovered a web page dedicated to the subject. Since then, he's learned so much he sometimes surprises me with forensic terminology I've heard only on TV series. I have to confess it's a shared interest: extreme, gratuitous, unpunished, cruel, perversely poetic violence is one of my recurring themes.

In my adolescence, I too compulsively read the stories and legends related to serial killers. From experience, I know that below the morbid patina coating these stories, there's a constant test of empathy and the moral limits of the imagination, a compassionate gaze. One is moved by the story of a logical sequence (the planning of a murder, the psychoanalytic inferences, and the forensic elements that allow the case to be solved), while being alternately repulsed and seduced by the concrete details of the execution, voids of meaning beyond their pornographic surface. I've experienced that ambiguous instinct. I'm terrified by the possibility of having passed on a disturbing tendency to my son. In some dark corner of my consciousness is the weariness of having battled for the past thirty years with the sociopathic streak left by my childhood.

One of the reasons I haven't been a good father is the puritanical self-obsession with which I perceive the bonds between my children and myself. A while ago, when Jorge was still in elementary school, Aída phoned me in alarm:

"The boy completely lost it at school. He pushed one of his classmates around, and even bashed his head against the wall."

The whole way there, I told myself that it was my fault. I'd done something very bad to my baby. I remembered how I used to cradle him crooning "The Chorus of the Hebrew Slaves," remixed with "By the Rivers of Babylon." I'd always liked the similarity of argument and tone between the two pieces. At that moment, however, they seemed more like lullabies fit for a monster: the biblical psalm on which they are both based ends with this verse: "Happy is the one who seizes your infants and dashes them against the rocks."

In the end, it turned out to be something less spectacular and obvious: other kids were bullying Jorge because he didn't live with his father. They branded him an orphan. His anger finally boiled over into violence.

Until I met Mónica, I viewed reproduction as a megalomaniacal theodicy. My birth seemed to me an act of pure personal evil that could only be atoned for by engendering another life. It's an idea I acquired from my mother, who considered her own life to be condemned and wretched (as decreed by my grandmother) except for the fact of having given birth to my siblings and me. Continuing this criminal lucubration, I began wanting to be a father at the age of seventeen. It was a fairly unfocused desire that started with an impossible sense of responsibility: unhealthy levels of output, burning the midnight oil. Throughout my last semester of high school, I stayed up until early morning listening to the radio, monitoring and analyzing information for the PRI and the government, a shameful task for which I earned decent money. Shortly after graduating, I enrolled in two college courses, and accepted—prematurely—the task of teaching writing in an unregistered high school that offered its illegal teachers a pittance. I decided to become a paterfamilias: for almost two years, I prohibited my mother from going to brothels; I was going to be the breadwinner. I organized the household responsibilities, apportioning them equally between her and my two brothers. The result was that, before the age of twenty, I'd had several bust-ups with Saíd, and Mamá and my sister were undernourished.

In addition to putting these bizarre keys to social success into practice, I decided to fall in love with only older single women willing to have unprotected sex. The lover who fit these requirements was Aída Guadalupe, an amateur actress, five years my senior. I suggested we live together. Mamá was furious:

"If you want to move in with that frigging bitch, fine: do it. But she'll make your life hell. And you're abandoning me, the person who's taken so much shit to get you this far. If you've already made up your mind, go ahead. But you're not my son anymore, you bastard, you're nothing but a mad dog."

I conquered paternity at the age of twenty-one. Then, when I was twenty-two, we separated.

The story could have ended there: a kid saved from the iniquity of the whorehouses of his childhood by a plump little baby. But then I met Sonia. Nineteen. A secretary. Putting herself through high school at night. She'd once had a boyfriend—I never met him—who, according to her, looked just like Luis Miguel. In soap-opera jargon, this boyfriend disappeared off the scene after *taking her virginity*. Sonia began coming to my rented room every day just after noon. Our meetings consisted of long fucks while talking about her boyfriend. We had a brilliant year.

Before I met her, I'd slept with five or six other women. Sex, for me, had been a transaction: something not so different from prostitution or paternity. In contrast, with Sonia, I discovered the civic depth of eroticism, that thing Mamá was unconsciously referring to one afternoon when, as we were walking together beside the long, long brick wall of La Huerta, she said:

"Lobo y Melón used to play here."

We did it with agility, but without any grand pirouettes. It's not that we were magnificent lovers: it just took us a long time to grow out of adolescence, and we were still graduating in the sport of slowness. There was a therapeutic subtlety in those first cleansing orgasms, the limpid gust of health imposing its unrhetorical aroma on my arrogant, poor-boy's solemnity, and the whiff of Catholic prudery my lover exuded each time, raising and turning her neck, she murmured:

"Don't think badly of me."

One day in December '93, she showed up later than usual. She'd brought the test kit with her: she was pregnant. I've no idea what I said in response. I do remember that the minute she left, I locked myself in the communal bathroom and stayed there for hours, looking in the mirror, grimacing and trying to count the pores on my face. I heard the bangs coming from outside as if from a specter I had no access to. After a while, someone kicked in the door, punched me a few times, and dragged me to my room.

So (or so I now feel: the past is made up of broken pulleys), at the age of twenty-three, I found myself sexually enthralled, earning a miserable wage, and the father of two children. I was sad to note I'd failed in my attempt to escape from home: I was a specimen worthy of inclusion in the diary of a sociology student evaluating the lives of young men descended from prostitutes.

"I don't know why you always have to do this," said Arturo.

"Do what?"

"Go off thinking your own things."

Only fifteen, but he's already as tall as me. He's very slim and handsome and, setting aside his fall from grace with serial killers, has what his family calls "a good heart." A long time ago, he invited me to his eighth-birthday celebration. It wasn't a very happy event: his mother had organized a party at a water park, but Arturo had fallen off his bicycle a couple of days before and broken his arm. As he couldn't play with his friends in the swimming pool, we spent a good part of the afternoon talking. He wanted to know about something the priest was always bringing up: free will. I tried to explain it honestly, convinced if we got through that, talking about sex in the future would be a cinch. I don't remember how our conversation ended. I only have the image of Arturo saying good-bye from the other side of a chain-link fence, waving, with some difficulty, his cast. That is the most intense bond between my children and me: a plastered wave good-bye.

Sonia emerged from the ministry.

"The passport guy wants to talk to you."

"Let's go," Arturo volunteered.

"No," she replied. "You stay here."

But we were both already heading for the building.

The passport guy explained that my identification papers were invalid.

"If you'd brought them a month ago, there'd have been no problem. But they've just changed our delegate, and you know how each official has his own institutional policy."

He lowered his voice.

"What I'd suggest is that you go to the Department of Transportation and take out a driver's license in your old name. I don't think they ask for more than 500 pesos on the side."

Arturo was standing next to me, his elbows on the counter. I said:

"First, I can't drive. And second, that's corruption."

"No, sir. Don't misunderstand me. I'm not asking for anything."

"It's corruption. And you go and blurt it out in front of my son."

Without another word, the official turned and disappeared through a door.

I caught my son's resentful gaze.

"It's always the same with you."

"You don't have to ask for money to be corrupt."

He turned his back on me and snarled:

"And you don't have to be a genius to get a frigging driver's license."

3

Mónica wakes at eight in the morning.

[I should have written *woke*. In fact I'm writing, hurriedly, from a plane over the Atlantic, trying to ensure that my laptop battery lasts through to the end of this long digression. Mónica keeps distracting me: she wants me to look out the window, down below, at something that could be Greenland, or any old piece of black rock abandoned in the snow. But that was then: now Mónica is looking annoyed and ashamed because I've asked her not to interrupt me. But that's gone too: now I look at her out of the corner of my eye, and she smiles with that pout of absolute availability and her enchanting, illegitimate princess of the House of Bourbon beauty that makes me want to undress her without worrying about her enormous pregnant belly or the fact that the tiny airplane seats are like the plastic chairs in a day nursery. But that's gone too: now . . .

Whenever you write in the present—whether to recount your airport cretinism, or your overdose of carbohydrates from the British Airways menu—you're generating a fiction, an involuntary suspension of grammatical disbelief. That's why this book (if this does become a book, if my mother survives or dies in some syntactical fold that restores the meaning of my digressions) will be eventually found in bookstores, standing upright on the dustiest shelf of "novels." I always narrate in the present in the hope of finding velocity. This time I'm doing it in the hope of finding consolation, while I perceive the progress of the plane through the sky as a free fall into an abyss on pause.]

Mónica wakes at eight in the morning. In no time at all, we shower, pack our bag, and pay our bill at the front desk of the Mandala. It's only eleven. Our plane leaves at four. We're being picked up at two. We decide to spend the few euros and couple of hours we have left on a quick cab ride—obviously, we're tourists—around our favorite stretch of Berlin: Unter den Linden from the Brandenburg Gate to Alexanderplatz. We want to re-experience the acrid, distilled smell of the lime trees that give the city its characteristic feel of slow, dense, whitish summer . . . The ride doesn't go well. The cab driver tries to explain to us in his guttural, impatient English that the most practical route for getting to our destination is along the side streets that are like the armored back of an intergalactic insect: long blue walls without windows, road surfaces under repair with red-and-white signs and protective meshing, the back door of the comic opera guarded by dark rectangles of glass. To top it all off, the radio is playing Bob Marley's "Buffalo Soldier." The idyllic nostalgia we're hoping to inject into our farewell to Berlin is forever tinged with the scent of the marijuana we used to smoke at seventeen. Annoyed, laughing, we get out of the cab and pay in coins and insults (in Spanish; the cab driver is surely returning them in his native tongue). We stand there, on some stretch of sidewalk, not knowing where to go, deeply embarrassed, confined to the imperfection of memory, the unarticulated eloquence of the sensory layers beneath every enunciation, layers that can only be glimpsed when you stop talking, close your eyes, and float down the river of adversity . . . The richest experience of the past (it makes no difference if it's personal or historical) is achieved by abandoning yourself to the physical perception of time: an instant always in the future. That's why guilt and nostalgia are paltry emotions.

Once, during Mamá's stay in the hospital, I spent seventy-two hours at her side. The first thing I did when I got home was to take a long shower. Mónica left me to it, without saying a word. Then we lay down and turned off the light. Mónica was serious, awake, her back to me. There was tension in the air between us, the nature of which was unclear to me at the time, but which I can now describe as a great love with the door latch removed.

"Can't you sleep?" I asked idiotically.

"I want to have a baby. Now," she said, turning to me.

Mónica and I met four years ago. We fell into bed, and spent hours there, hardly even bothering to tell each other our names, and long before having a coherent conversation. Sex between us was an intuition of luminosity. Sex—the simplest and most perfect thing to which you can aspire, like drinking pure water without paying for the PET bottle—is what revealed the visceral bond between us, more solid than any other commitment we had to the world. A bond so deep that, in my nightmares, it seemed like incest.

After a week, we decided to move in together. A couple of months afterward, she left her job at a television station, packed up her home in the capital, started divorce proceedings, and moved to my city. I left my bachelor apartment, sobered up, and got an office job. Later, we bought a house: a petit bourgeois gesture I found repugnant for years, but that, seen in the light of my passion for Mónica, was completely natural.

Before the night we decided to become parents, our union was based on two reconciliations: she became reconciled with her body, and I with my continued existence. I don't know how it was for her, but my reconciliation was a matter of survival. A year before I met her, I'd attempted—with more rage and theatricality than conscious intention—to commit suicide. I'd received a hundred thousand pesos as a prize for a book. I bought several bottles of bourbon and three ounces of cocaine, locked the door, and threw away the key for a couple of weeks. I wanted to snort till I dropped. My plan was based on a mixture of frivolity and defeat—I wonder if those words are in fact synonyms—because, after ten minutes of fame, I managed to get a glimpse of the limits of my writing. It wasn't, naturally, a reflective space. It was this paragraph: experiences that are incommunicable, not for being ecstatic, but for their carcinogenic qualities.

I don't know how long we would have been able to go on like that, impermeable to the void. I suppose a few years more. But when leukemia began to eat away at Mamá's body, it also contaminated, in a superficial, pestilential way, the invisible organism within which my wife and I floated. If you spend your time caring for a sick person, you risk living in the interior of a corpse.

Then Mónica said that stuff about the baby.

My first reaction was panic. My ego was already feeling pretty undermined by the prospect of spending who knows how long on a diet of the meager pleasures involved in protecting the remains of an aged, moribund prostitute. And it was now being suggested that I, once again, advance along the rain-swept highway of paternity. The topic of pregnancy: another way of saying graceless sex, nocturnal discomforts, new hospital experiences. The postnatal stage: *the baby*, that tyrannical, lovely subspecies, a sacred shark of the mind that, on the route to education and enlightenment, can very well devour you. But, above all, the sense of mourning I've been living with since the age of twenty-four: the certainty of having failed as a father on two occasions. The certainty of being, for someone I love and who is alive, simply a self-conscious nerve in pain.

Long before concluding my mental survey of the cons, I made my decision.

"Sure," I said.

Not to please her. I discovered reproduction was the only exercise of will my body retained. I wanted to settle accounts with the mother goddess of biology, shooting a pistol at her, ejaculating in her face. When all is said and done, one is scarcely a tiny creature emerging from prehistoric caverns, and the horror of death can only be alleviated by a statistical cleansing. And so it was that, while Mamá was lying in room 101 of the Saltillo University Hospital, Mónica and I were agreeing to create a substitute for her life by draining out a couple of its warts. A couple of viscous warts we elected to christen Leonardo, a name that, for us, had hints of absolute brilliance, a French art gallery, and missile engineering.

Three months into the pregnancy, we received an e-mail from Germany inviting us, again, for a reading.

We landed in Berlin on a Thursday afternoon, accompanied by a majestic belly that threw the cabin crews and customs officials of four countries off track. Due to the transfers, we'd been traveling for twenty-four hours. We turned up briefly for the welcome drinks and by seven were sleeping in the Hotel Mandala. *Sleeping in a mandala*. The dawn light woke us at exactly four, and we went out onto the balcony. The street was deserted. Across from us—the first time we'd seen it—was the roof of the Sony Center: a sort of aerial labyrinth or gigantic shrouded kite. The banner advertisements and red lettering of the cinema. And lower down, hidden in a nook, the face of Albert Einstein, in gray and white pieces, looking at us from the window of the Lego store.

[It was perhaps at that moment, or a little afterward, while Mónica was putting a sweater on over her pajamas, and we were going swiftly down in the elevator to see the giraffe and Einstein's face close up, that the topic and structure of this section occurred to me: paternity as a redemptive strangeness; legacy as a Lego model with pieces always missing.]

"Shall we go see?" asked Mo.

She put a sweater on over her pajamas and we rode the elevator down to the street. We crossed the empty road and headed directly for Albert's dark plastic eyes. Behind the glass of the store window, under the vigilance of the most venerable mustache in the history of physics, lay half-constructed toys: miniature gray fire engines next to yellow cranes, blue airplanes, green zoos, characters from a bizarre *Star Wars*, Power Miners, Duplos, and, in a place of honor, on a shelf, almost level with Albert's left eye, an NXT robot, assembled in the classic humanoid form. Scarcely a week before, Mónica and I had bought Leonardo his first book: an introductory manual on robotics with a photograph of this same toy on the cover.

Outside, on the sidewalk, the designers from the store had constructed a Lego sculpture, an almost ironic version of the equestrian statue of Frederick the Great on Unter den Linden: a giraffe, over fifteen feet high, carefully assembled from yellow and brown cubes. It's a popular giraffe because, as I later learned, tourists have stolen the prick on a number of occasions, and a squad of operatives has had to reconstruct it.

"Stand under it," said Mónica. "This is going to be your first photo of the trip."

"Julián Herbert dies, crushed by the giraffe of the ego."

The first days of summer slip by so fast. Especially if you're traveling with an almost-four-pound fetus in your belly.

Now we're standing on a stretch of sidewalk, somewhere near Potsdamerplatz, seriously insulting the cab driver who has driven us so badly, singing silently to ourselves, "And he was taken from Africa, brought to America." Our plane will be leaving soon, there's no time now to take a carriage ride along Unter den Linden, as the nobility used to. Confused, not knowing who to ask for directions, we walk toward where I think our hotel is, and where Mónica calculates we'll see the Brandenburg Gate.

Neither of us is right: we reach the entrance to th garten through a small esplanade covered with gray t Years ago, someone had told me about this place. A squa what resembles concrete tombs to commemorate the mil Jews who had had to confront Hitler's insanity. It hadr occurred to me to look for it on the map. And here it was three blocks from the hotel. A mandala of irregular rect My first impression as we wander into the symbolic lal is solemn. I feel it isn't death that walks here, but son moribund: spirituality (but I don't fuckin' care). Over th tion, another more precise one grows. I remember som maybe Timo Berger—telling me on my first visit to Ber the monument was a piece of nerve: it was constructe a special type of anti-graffiti coating produced by a C company whose capital had been amassed by nothing le the dispossession of Jews during the Third Reich. Th other layer of perception, lighter and sharper: walking hand with my pregnant lady through a labyrinth relat graveyard. We three—always *three*—are now a metapho Mystery, a set of Lego pieces around a belly, a spherica phage en route to being expelled toward life while the of the concrete blocks rises like a tide and is already lev my shoulders, and now above my head, and is like an c residential tower blocks completed by that great whor who has lately been hanging around at all hours, and i istential Lego model whose historical significance is e by the naked horror of form. Berlin isn't a wall. Berlin i graveyard project into which has been drained the be sacred art: dead bodies.

But beneath it all, beneath the final urban halluc while the height of the blocks ebbs and we can gradual out, beyond the gray swell, the greenery of the Tierg have an epiphany: this was the first dream I'd had in

"Shall we go see?" asked Mo.

She put a sweater on over her pajamas and we rode the elevator down to the street. We crossed the empty road and headed directly for Albert's dark plastic eyes. Behind the glass of the store window, under the vigilance of the most venerable mustache in the history of physics, lay half-constructed toys: miniature gray fire engines next to yellow cranes, blue airplanes, green zoos, characters from a bizarre *Star Wars*, Power Miners, Duplos, and, in a place of honor, on a shelf, almost level with Albert's left eye, an NXT robot, assembled in the classic humanoid form. Scarcely a week before, Mónica and I had bought Leonardo his first book: an introductory manual on robotics with a photograph of this same toy on the cover.

Outside, on the sidewalk, the designers from the store had constructed a Lego sculpture, an almost ironic version of the equestrian statue of Frederick the Great on Unter den Linden: a giraffe, over fifteen feet high, carefully assembled from yellow and brown cubes. It's a popular giraffe because, as I later learned, tourists have stolen the prick on a number of occasions, and a squad of operatives has had to reconstruct it.

"Stand under it," said Mónica. "This is going to be your first photo of the trip."

"Julián Herbert dies, crushed by the giraffe of the ego."

The first days of summer slip by so fast. Especially if you're traveling with an almost-four-pound fetus in your belly.

Now we're standing on a stretch of sidewalk, somewhere near Potsdamerplatz, seriously insulting the cab driver who has driven us so badly, singing silently to ourselves, "And he was taken from Africa, brought to America." Our plane will be leaving soon, there's no time now to take a carriage ride along Unter den Linden, as the nobility used to. Confused, not knowing who to ask for directions, we walk toward where I think our hotel is, and where Mónica calculates we'll see the Brandenburg Gate.

Neither of us is right: we reach the entrance to the Tiergarten through a small esplanade covered with gray tumuli. Years ago, someone had told me about this place. A square with what resembles concrete tombs to commemorate the millions of Jews who had had to confront Hitler's insanity. It hadn't even occurred to me to look for it on the map. And here it was, barely three blocks from the hotel. A mandala of irregular rectangles. My first impression as we wander into the symbolic labyrinth is solemn. I feel it isn't death that walks here, but something moribund: spirituality (but I don't fuckin' care). Over that emotion, another more precise one grows. I remember someone—maybe Timo Berger—telling me on my first visit to Berlin that the monument was a piece of nerve: it was constructed using a special type of anti-graffiti coating produced by a German company whose capital had been amassed by nothing less than the dispossession of Jews during the Third Reich. Then another layer of perception, lighter and sharper: walking hand in hand with my pregnant lady through a labyrinth related to a graveyard. We three—always *three*—are now a metaphor of the Mystery, a set of Lego pieces around a belly, a spherical sacrophage en route to being expelled toward life while the height of the concrete blocks rises like a tide and is already level with my shoulders, and now above my head, and is like an ocean of residential tower blocks completed by that great whore death who has lately been hanging around at all hours, and is an existential Lego model whose historical significance is exceeded by the naked horror of form. Berlin isn't a wall. Berlin is a civic graveyard project into which has been drained the best of its sacred art: dead bodies.

But beneath it all, beneath the final urban hallucination, while the height of the blocks ebbs and we can gradually make out, beyond the gray swell, the greenery of the Tiergarten, I have an epiphany: this was the first dream I'd had in Europe.

The first time around, before passing through Tegel airport: walking without landscape through a cemetery of Führers, each one interred in his bunker of choice.

"Do you want a photo?" Mónica asks.

I don't reply.

So we don't take one last tourist shot among the dark stone rectangles. Beyond the landscape. Beyond the present. A few yards before we enter the Animal Forest.

The Saltillo University Hospital (formerly the Civilian Hospital) was opened in 1951. It was designed in 1943 by the Mexican architect and urbanist Mario Pani, famous for his predilection for the ideas of Le Corbusier and for having planned both the Juárez apartment complex and another block in Nonoalco Tlatelolco: projects that now symbolize the destruction caused by the 1985 earthquake.

The history of the U.H. is (as the old people say, wagging an arthritic finger before your face) "inextricably bound up with the history of Mexico." Not for its architectural merit, much less its role in the field of medicine, but because its surprising origin is a good example of Mexicans' great talent for making themselves look foolish.

It all began with the Nazis.

As is well known, the Nazis conspired for years across the length and breadth of our Sweet Nation, seducing, intriguing, longing to set up what would be, given our proximity to the United States, strategic military bases. It's also well known that the Nazis needed our oil (*our*, what a mannerist word, now it's all going down the drain, now the real gold doesn't come from underground, but from the jungles of Colombia, and the teeth of Kalashnikovs rattle all afternoon against the wall while Felipe Calderón drools on his tie). But that's not all: it's also known that Hilde Krüger (ex-actress, Goebbels's former lover, and

Abwehr agent) thumped thighs, first with the influential politician Ramón Beteta, and then with the future president, Miguel Alemán, both of whom served in Manuel Ávila Camacho's government between 1940 and 1946. It's said that Hilde did it for the sole purpose of promoting and fomenting Hitler's cause within our ideological spectrum. I've no doubt this is true. But neither does it seem to me an extraordinary triumph for a pair of thighs: using fascist arguments to indoctrinate Mexican politicians in positions of power is preaching to the converted. On the other hand, it's not irrelevant to mention the fortunes generated by nationalism within the nation's business community. In Saltillo, no less, one present-day working-class neighborhood is called Guayulera. It owes this name to an old rubber factory whose owners got rich providing the German army with tires.

At the beginning of the Second World War, the Ávila Camacho regime maintained—more from sloth and simple-mindedness than for ideological reasons—neutrality, although with evident sympathy for the Allies. Then, during the summer of '42 (when my grandmother Juana discovered, to her horror, that she was pregnant with my mother), German submarines sank six Mexican oil tankers that were supplying a number of their U.S. counterparts in the Gulf of Mexico. In thunderous retaliation, the Mexican government declared war on the Axis powers. The relevant ministry pulled from its sleeve its highest-caliber weapon: the 201st Mexican Fighter Squadron, also known as the Aztec Eagles.

The story of the 201st Squadron is like something from a satirical novel by Jorge Ibargüengoitia.

After the declaration of hostilities, the Mexican government took three years (1942–1945) to ready an impressive army of two hundred ninety-nine men, of whom no more than thirty-six could be strictly considered weapons of war: fighter pilots. There were two simple reasons for the delay: Mexican soldiers lacked training, and our bureaucracy has been slow since its infancy. Before sending off his squadron, Ávila Camacho had to sign heaps of decrees that included the creation of the Air Force, various official name changes, applications to the senate, and so on. The group finally went into action on June 17, 1945. And it seems they didn't do badly. Unfortunately, their mission came to an end on August 26 of the same year, not long before the Japanese surrender. We Mexicans should use this chronology as a mathematical table for calculating national productivity: three years of bureaucracy is equivalent to two and a half months of concrete policy.

The members of the 201st Squadron were trained in the United States, but not by other combatants: they received their instruction from the WASP: Women Airforce Service Pilots; a highly professional group, progressive in terms of their working practices and ideology, but without combat experience, who were, of course, no favorites with the machos like Greg "Pappy" Boyington, who controlled the North American army. (In fact the WASP disappeared in '44, and it wasn't until 1970 that they won the status of Second World War veterans.) All this speaks eloquently of what the aviators of the neighboring country thought of our pilots. I can't be certain they were wrong: but in any case, why was it better not to allow the WASP to fight?

Of the thirty-six original Mexican pilots, two died during the first training sessions and six were discharged on medical grounds (the writer Marcelo Yarza claims, without offering sources or proof, that they failed the drug tests). After a couple of replacements, the 201st eventually consisted of thirty aviators who left for the front in the Philippines . . . Without planes. The P-47 Thunderbolts belonging to Mexico—which the Aztec Eagles should have piloted—never arrived in the combat zone. Our compatriots had—once again—to borrow. Can you guess from whom? The North American army provided eighteen fighter planes, and even tolerated the Mexican flag flying next to the Stars and Stripes. But twelve of the pilots belonging to the squadron never left the ground. Which really made them Phantom pilots.

The whole escapade cost the country seven lives and three million dollars, at least half of which would have been better spent if someone had dropped the bills like leaflets over the mountains of Oaxaca.

But I digress: What does the 201st Squadron have to do with my mother, leukemia, infusion pumps, and the opening—in 1951, with a design by Mario Pani—of the Civilian Hospital, now the Saltillo University Hospital?

Shortly after the president informed the Mexican citizenry that they were at war with Germany, Italy, and Japan, a group of businessmen from Saltillo got together to discuss the matter (I guess, given the outcome, this chat must have taken place in a cantina). Scarcely interested in what was happening within their own community, but dismayed by the fate of the world, the businessmen decided it was their civic duty to support the president in this epic adventure. Between them, they collected a million pesos and sent them to Manuel Ávila Camacho with a note stating that the sum should be put toward the military budget. Ávila Camacho—who must have been very busy, and in a bad temper, his hand numb from signing so many air force decrees—snubbed them: he returned the gift, saying it would be better to invest their resources in something that would benefit the city in which they lived. The story, sadly, makes no mention of the foot-stamping tantrums of the bellicose Saltillo businessmen. But there is a record of the fate of those million pesos: they were used to start work on what is now the U.H.

Poetic justice.

I don't know if Mario Pani was aware of the aeronautical delusions that gave rise to his project. But the truth is that, seen from above, the building he designed for my city is shaped like a plane suffering from degenerative disease: the snub nose, short, thin wings, a slender fuselage, and a chubby tail. Even the lobby, from a pedestrian's viewpoint, looks like the flying saucer of a Leninist extraterrestrial. And what's more, the interior distribution of space bears a resemblance to the *Battlestar Galactica*.

The hospital faces north. To the east and west of the lobby (that is to say, of the flying saucer) stretch two-story annexes: wings. The west wing houses oncology and radiotherapy; the east is occupied by the ER. The upper floors are offices. The main body of the building, with three floors and a basement, is to the south (from the air, we could say in the tail of the plane). To get there from the flying saucer, it's necessary to ascend ten steps and traverse a long, narrow corridor, very like those in science fiction movies connecting the bridge to the main deck. This corridor—along one of its walls is a minimuseum illustrating the evolution of medical technology through a beautiful collection of surgical instruments—leads to a second reception area with elevators and a waiting room equipped with a television set and hideous blue armchairs. The southern section covers almost the whole medical spectrum: from maternity to intensive care, and even the morgue, located, of course, in the basement. On either side of the edifice, courtyards were constructed. While the eastern one has been almost completely engulfed by the parking lot, the western courtyard still retains its original design of tree-lined gardens, the ground covered by a mosaic of melon and deep red, and is in such a state of abandonment that it is an excellent spot to smoke and read when the night air is not too cold.

Male medical is on the first floor of the west deck of what I have termed "the tail": the southern end of the building.

There, in a corner of the starship, Mamá is fighting the second round of her personal war against leukemia.

With pyrrhic victories.

In December she was discharged. We celebrated with a *taquizo* on her birthday. Then, at the end of February, she was deeply moved to hear that Mónica was pregnant. She practically forced Diana to give us some blankets and the cradle that had belonged to my nieces.

Then, in mid-June, while Mónica and I were in Berlin, Mamá was readmitted: the leukemia had floored her once again, as was to be expected. At her express request, the doctors agreed to allot her the room she'd had before.

History repeated itself: sleepless nights at her bedside and weeks of poison. After the last chemo session of this second round, the body of Señora "Charles" went into remission again. They showed her blood count to Valencia, suggesting she could go home in a few days. The optimism lasted only a couple of hours: that night her temperature rose to 104. We had to stuff her with Tylenol and put bags of ice under her legs and the back of her neck. The following morning we tried another blood test. After a thorough examination, I was called out of the room and given an explanation:

"It's not up to us now. Lupita has caught a nosocomial infection. We don't know what it is or where she picked it up. We'll go on treating her with broad-spectrum antibiotics."

Second base: infection.

Fever must be one of our most commonly used metonyms. In it, the symptoms of withdrawal from hard drugs and viral hallucination coexist. Hitler's destruction, the bureaucratic megalomania of Mexican presidents, the civic narcissism of a small-town businessman, the visions of an architect who designs hospitals in the shape of a mother ship. Mystical purity. Thomas Mann spying on adolescents in the lobby of a Zurich hotel and Alexis Texas modeling fluorescent swimwear for Bang Bros and Vincent Vega dancing with Mia Wallace, internally connected to the syringe. The agony or extreme cruelty of old sick people beneath dirty blankets. All the cold, all the heat, the toxic water sweated out in a bed. Almost all of it always in a bed. In a bed or on the verge of collapse. There's no route to the absolute that doesn't pass through a fever station.

As a child I used to like having a fever. It was a condition that made Mamá particularly affectionate. One of my earliest favorite texts is a very short story in verse by Stevenson in which a sick child designs military strategies on the mountain chains formed by his legs under the sheets. Mamá would read this to me, or *The Little Prince*, or "The Little Florentine Scribe" while I was burning up. She would touch her lips to my forehead, bring me chicken soup, carry me in her arms to the bathroom. I pay her back now checking the expiration dates of her drugs and lulling her to sleep with Puerto Rican or Cuban songs: I haven't seen Linda, can hardly believe it. Because I'm her son. I'm no mad dog.

At eight in the morning, a nun comes in and puts a gram of Tylenol in the infusion pump. At ten past eight, she returns, disconnects everything, and explains she's put the wrong drug in: this is the interchangeable generic version and we'd bought a branded product. She changes the mixture, reconnects the pump, and leaves. The pump begins to beep almost immediately. Someone comes to fix it, but the machine switches itself off exactly every ten minutes for over an hour, until the head nurse arrives and supplants technology with a piece of Mexicanicity: she measures out the dose by rule of thumb. I don't trust this system, so I spend the next hour watching the solution drip from the bottle into the IV tubing: one drop every thirty seconds. I use Mamá's cell phone to time the drips and it turns out the nurse had calculated the positioning of the roller clamp with spine-chilling accuracy. Around midday, a mature, well-built care assistant comes and stops the drip again. She explains that the best way to lower the fever is by taking a shower. Let's get on with it, she says, nodding toward my mother's scrawny body. I explain I'd prefer to leave the task until my sister arrives. But the assistant, who is taller than me and must weigh twenty pounds more, firmly claps me on the back and says: Come on, you're not a man now, you're a loving son, don't let me down. I carry the limp body, undress it, and, with a bit of a balancing act, put it in the shower. Mamá's nipples emit that characteristic plastic stink that bodies marinated in the rancid vinegar of chemicals exude, plus something I've inwardly christened "the excipient unit dose smell." She lowers her eyelids and whispers, "Twenty inches, twenty inches." When I'm about to turn on the water, the internal medicine team shows up on their daily round. They practically snatch her from my arms and cover her with a gown again. They beg me to leave the room while they examine her, "showing all due respect." Outside, one of the general medicine students, a woman who sometimes flirts with me, offers me a coffee and suggests I don't try the shower again: when a patient can't manage on her own, it's the job of the hospital staff to help. On the other side of the corridor, the well-built care assistant is standing at the door to the nurses' bathroom. Each time the medical student turns away she frowns at me and rotates the palm of her left hand back and forth at chest level. Her lips silently articulate the classic, ambiguous threat: "You'll see, you'll see . . ." I'm called back into the room, asked to force Mamá to take her dose of Ensure each morning. Mamá generally spits out most of the dietary supplement onto her gown and my shirtsleeves. The doctors call a nurse and ask her to bathe Mamá and put on clean clothes while they exchange opinions in a technical language supposedly incomprehensible to the layman, but that, by now, seems just pedantic. The general medicine student comes into the room, sits down next to me on the sofa, puts a hand on my thigh, and looks straight into my eyes until I feel uncomfortable. Suddenly, without any measurable transition, a doctor I've never seen before turns and says:

"Things are going well, eh? Don't worry. There's been no change, which, in this case, should be considered good news."

They leave.

Shortly afterward, the youngest doctor returns. Dr. O.

He says:

"I just want to check . . ."

He examines her again, concentrating on the area around the back of her left shoulder.

"She's got fluid on that lung. I'm thinking of removing it by making a surgical incision and inserting a tube under the clavicle. What do you think . . . ?"

Most of the doctors do not consider me a thinking being: they just give me instructions. Dr. O., in contrast, talks to me as if I were one of his colleagues. I understand he does this out of deference to my humanity, that essence of which, through the last months, has been hijacked by what was once a woman and is now a useless old rag. I understand, but refuse to tolerate it. Maintaining a dialogue with me based on the principle of free choice is a lamentable assault on etiquette.

"It's up to you," I reply with a shrug.

He addresses me informally, like a friend. I speak to him formally, like an elder, even though he's ten years younger than me.

Another doctor enters without knocking. I don't know his name: he comes around only occasionally. He's very tall and, although he also seems young, is almost completely bald.

"Still trying?" he says irritably.

"She has to be aspirated," responds Dr. O.

"It's not your decision. Valencia has already given instructions." Then, turning to me, "Have they brought you the prescription?"

"No. I haven't been given any prescription."

For several hours, the doctors go back and forth over the issue of draining the liquid that has taken up residence in her lung. One comes in and asks, "Hasn't the porter come for her yet . . . ?" and goes back out without waiting for an answer. Five minutes later, the bald one reappears: "Don't allow them to take her until we have authorization from the hematologist." I feel like I'm trapped in a Marx Brothers movie. Finally the hematologist rings Mamá's cell phone and gives me a direct order: no one is to do anything until there's been another case review.

A few minutes after that, the bald one returns to our room, wearing an expression of bureaucratic triumph.

"Has the hematologist spoken to you?"

I nod.

"So we'll leave it at that, right?"

I nod again.

"Have they brought the prescription yet?"

"No. They haven't brought the prescription."

"Don't worry. It'll be here soon."

The procedure for obtaining medicines in the U.H. goes like this:

1. The doctors order medication at the nurses' station.
2. The prescription is passed to a family member.
3. The patient's family member goes to the social work area, where someone approves the documentation.
4. The patient's family member returns to the nurses' station and asks one of them (the majority refuse this request) to sign the paper and add his or her identity card number.
5. With this data and the prescription, the patient's family member goes to the pharmacy and hands his request to the dispenser.

6. The dispenser gives an estimated price.
7. The estimated price is taken by the patient's family member back to the social work office to be stamped.
8. Back at the pharmacy with the stamped document, the member of the patient's family is given the medication.
9. The medication then has to be handed in at the nurses' station by the member of the patient's family.
10. For the handover to be official, the person who receives the medication from the member of the patient's family must be the same one who signed the order and authorized it with his or her identity card number.

The whole thing takes an hour or two, depending on the length of the line in each department.

I doubt the U.H. imposed these rules from either administrative ineptitude or bureaucratic cruelty. In fact, I think they do it out of pragmatic solidarity: time here passes at a snail's pace. The Kafkaesque procedure for obtaining medication is their version of occupational therapy.

(All of a sudden Émil Cioran's little books on antipersonal development for adolescents come to mind. The one, for example, in which insomnia reveals to him the most profound sense of the trouble with existence: it impelled him toward unlimited spite: walking to the shoreline and throwing stones at some poor seagulls. Jeez, what a punk. For me—also a chronic insomniac—the condition is pure melodrama: just an unshackled state of mind. At most, it makes you a little cynical. No: the real inconvenience of having been born doesn't lie in some unified meaning that can be narrated. It is rather this perpetual cold turkey of structure, these withdrawal symptoms of signification. The desire to symbolize everything, the anguished need to convert anodyne stories into prose. For example, bureaucratic red tape, whose inquisitorial in-significance is the nearest thing to the *Malleus Maleficorum* medieval twenty-first-century Latin America has been able to put into practice.)

Occupational therapy.

The first week is the worst. The days seem like disemboweled Trojans. As if you were trying to read (or write) a novel for the first time, and what you found as you progressed were disturbing images, sentences impossible to reduce to a specific function within the story, unconnected scenes, febrile intonation. Then, gradually, boredom wins out. As if you'd spent hours watching a drop of Tempra fall into a tube. And you begin to see things with a time lag. The geometry of your enclosure. Its history, which silently settles out from very diverse sources. Articulation: the physiological epiphany that allows you to sense the precise places your voice comes from. The spectral nature of your characters when you manage to isolate them . . . Inhabiting something (or somebody) is acquiring a habit. And in that habit, those of us addicted to hard drugs have a certain advantage. I inhabit (I haunt) a hospital. Every new day of enclosure damages me organically, and at the same time it provides me with some necessary detail for the plans of my house.

a) The visitors' restrooms are outside, to one side of the flying saucer, opposite the entrance to the ER. You have to pay two pesos to use the facilities. They are supposed to be cleaned every four hours, but perpetually smell of shit and bleach. By tacit accord, pornographic magazines are always to be found under the waste bins in the men's room. You can flick through them, but afterward they are supposed to be replaced for the benefit of the next user. Not even the cleaning woman dares remove them. New issues invariably appear each Tuesday.
b) Every Friday, around eight, a family of bakers—the husband, his fat, blondly peroxided wife, their teenage daughter—

offer coffee and broken almond cookies to the people sleeping in the waiting room. Apparently, they have been coming for ten years without missing a single Friday.

c) At night an eight-year-old boy appears in the stairwell. It's easy to recognize him: he's got a hole in his head. I haven't seen him. "Naturally," one of the nuns on the nursing staff mutters reproachfully. "That's what unbelievers always say." It's rumored he was the victim of the famous *trenazo* of October 4, 1972: a train crash in which some three hundred people perished at Puente Moreno, to the south of Saltillo. And it's also rumored he survived the journey, but when the porter, pushing him at high speed to surgery, managed to upturn the stretcher, he was killed. And that's why his soul didn't rest in peace: it couldn't resign itself to having died in such an idiotic way.

d) The U.H.'s nocturnal pet is a stray dog the security guards call Chinto. He often dines on the contents of the garbage containers opposite the building. A woman whose husband has been in intensive care for over a month has given it a T-shirt with a picture of the state governor, Humberto Moreira, and the PRI logo. Chinto sometimes sneaks in through the door from the western courtyard and curls up in the short corridor between oncology and the flying saucer. If a doctor happens to see him, the security guards kick him (the dog) out. But if not, they leave him be, and even give him scraps of their food.

e) In the early morning, the U.H. is transformed into the *Event Horizon*: a ghost starship that has traveled through hell. The main entrance has been closed since ten at night. The security guards stay at their posts a few hours longer. Then their spirits begin to wane. Both the staff and some of the patients' relations gather in the ER (the only area open 24/7) to gossip, watch TV, or take a nap if there are any

> empty stretchers. The lobby, by contrast, is deserted. The night shift doctors retire to their hut, have a surreptitious drink, play cards. The nurses of both genders sleep, tune in to a reggaeton station on the radio, self-medicate in private, or smooch and have oral sex out of sheer boredom. It's just sport.

The early hours of the morning. Mamá was sleeping peacefully. I got the urge to go out for a smoke. Rain was falling in one of those downpours that make the pious say God is trying out his strategy for the next Flood in Saltillo. I went down to the first floor and hid in the turn of a concrete ramp between the nurses' office and the basement, along which bodies are transported from the upper floors to the dissecting room. It's the least busy area of the building, especially at night, and was at that moment in almost complete darkness. A thin strip of light filtered through from the nurses' office, accompanied by the murmuring of voices reading out numbers, and the mechanical tapping of a desk calculator. A little farther off, the glow of the stairwell by the elevators.

A slight noise came from the end of the corridor. Something like the sporadic, secret flapping of swing doors. A metallic but soft drumming that made me imagine the tension in a giant spring at the bottom of a swimming pool. As I was winding back and forth along the final section of the ramp, I wondered if; other than the charades that make the hospital personnel go soft in the head, there was any way to communicate with the dead bodies lying a few yards from me, behind the two aluminum sheets shielding the most recondite corner of the hospital: the morgue and the autopsy room.

With that morbid thought in mind, I approached the end of the ramp, passed the landing (on the right) and the nurses' office (on the left), and reached the door with its meager metallic gleam, taking the last section almost on tiptoe, as if hoping to surprise the faintest trace of breath in a corpse: baby's sighs. The clanking—I guessed they were admitting a new body—became more clearly defined as I moved closer. There was a familiar harmony in the sound; almost the prospect of language. I thought: perhaps this is how the dead communicate with each other. Porters and watchmen and pathologists develop precise movements, perfect anatomical mechanisms for dismantling a stretcher or unfolding a sheet, or carefully passing an inanimate torso from the mattress to the slab. A rhythmic, efficient routine whose deceptive obscenity hides the most solemn of funerary rituals.

I reached the threshold. Before peeking through, I turned and looked toward the light welling from the nurses' office behind me to confirm that I wasn't being spied on. There was no one there. I bent over slightly and put my ear to the aluminum rectangle. It was ice cold. It took me a few seconds to understand the message. Then, little by little, beneath the regular tapping, I began to distinguish human moans. The voice, that demon possessing us—says Slavoj Žižek—*between the body* . . . Someone on the other side of the door was fornicating, surrounded by corpses, but with enviable precision, perfect rhythm, pushing some part of his body against the edges of something unfixed and metallic: a set of shelves or maybe a stretcher.

I hesitated: Could it be a necrophiliac screwing the posthumous remains of a slim girl . . . ? I listened a little longer and decided that no: the moaning was in two distinct pitches. One deep, the other higher.

With repulsion, I noted my sense of alarm transforming into excitement. Two nights previously, at home, during one of my rest periods, I'd caught a Kate Winslet movie on cable, the one where she falls in love with a neighbor, a married man. For some reason, they both arrive at her house, drenched by a rain shower. Kate asks him for his shirt and goes down to the basement. He's alone for a few minutes. He takes a look around and when he finds a photo of himself in shorts, bare chested, beside a swimming pool, he realizes the woman finds him desirable. The image is inside a copy of Shakespeare's sonnets, a bookmark for a poem with a verse underlined in red: "My love is as a fever." The man goes down to the basement. He creeps up on Kate. Stands behind her. Massages her shoulders. Puts his arms around her. She turns and kisses him. He gently pushes her to the back of the room. He lifts her onto the washing machine, looks into her eyes. She undresses, rolling up her slip and pulling her dress over her head. Then she winds her legs around the man, while his back covers the whole frame, except for a glimpse of the beautiful, pronounced concavity between her rib cage and the slight suggestion of her hip. They fuck without human voice: the only sound is the slowish metallic rattling of the washing machine against the wall.

That was the image assaulting my brain for the minute or so I spent spying on the lovers with an ear flattened against the aluminum door of the morgue of the Saltillo University Hospital. I then straightened up—ashamed of myself—and walked toward the stairwell and the elevators. My palms were sweating. I had no idea where to go. The thought of spending the night in that state, watching over my sick mother, disgusted me.

I sat on the bottom step, lit another Marlboro, and decided I had to see her. It made no difference whether she was good-looking or plain, fat or thin or old. I had to wait there until they came out, and erase the image of Kate Winslet having an orgasm in a morgue from my mind.

Five, maybe ten minutes went by. The aluminum door opened. Two shadows emerged. The man was tall and wearing what seemed to be, in the darkness, a gown. The woman was slim, athletic, with nice breasts, and, since the external light illuminated the blue of her trousers, I knew she was one of the student residents. The man spotted me and walked over. She stayed in the darkest part of the corridor. I was able to make out his face from the light coming down the stairwell. He was a handsome, mature doctor. Almost certainly the specialist in charge of the area in which the wholesome girl with whom he had recently been cavorting was an intern.

"What are you doing here?"

The question took me by surprise.

"I came down for a smoke," I replied honestly.

The man looked at me for a second. Then he went back to the girl, whispered something, and the two of them walked down the corridor away from me. I was able to catch only a glimpse of her head in the dim glow from the nurses' office. I couldn't describe her face.

I was about to make my departure when I heard someone coming down the stairs behind me. The heavy, uneven steps reached me. Then a hand rested on my shoulder. I stood up and turned around. Overhead, as a backdrop, the lightning flashes of a storm entered through the window on the landing.

"Let me have one?" said the newcomer, pointing to the pack of Marlboros in my shirt pocket.

I briefly studied him, perhaps imitating the inquiring look the doctor had previously directed at me. He was wearing an impeccable pair of Atletica sweatpants, black-and-orange New Balance sneakers, and a black T-shirt with the brand name Girbaud printed in plastic. He had a slight paunch, and shoulder-length, straggling, wavy hair: he was going bald.

"You can't smoke here," he said with a smile. "And it's forbidden to spy on dead people's sex lives, right?"

I was startled. I thought I'd bumped into one of the ghosts that terrified the nun. The guy took advantage of my confusion to extract the Marlboros from my shirt pocket with a neat, practiced snatch of the thumb and index finger of his right hand. He took a silver Zippo from his pants, lit a cigarette, pulled deeply on it, and blew out the smoke.

"Frigging doctors, dude. They're all the same. And the worst thing is the doors and the walls. They're so thin." He took another drag. "The day I came here, they gave me number 34. And in the next room there was a foreign couple. Incredible: so slovenly and loud. Every morning they used to go to it, making noises that were ill suited to the fresh morning: as if they were soiling it in some sultry way. It was a battle with smothered giggles and gasps, and I couldn't ignore the indelicate nature of it, much as I tried, out of kindheartedness, to find a harmless explanation for it. First it sounded as if they were playing at chasing each other around the furniture, but then it was obvious the game had turned bestial. And I thought, 'They must be ill, or at least one of them must be, since they're here. A bit of self-control wouldn't be out of place.' Don't you agree?"

His stiff, outdated speech seemed familiar: déjà vu. I tried to work out why, and soon figured it out. What the stranger had just said was taken, more or less, from one of the early scenes in *The Magic Mountain*: when Hans Castorp has his first unfortunate encounter with the Russian couple.

I looked him straight in the eye.

He held my gaze. Then he winked and added:

"Precisely."

After that, he went off in the direction of the morgue, walking in a familiar, comical way: waddling like a duck until he exited through the door leading to the parking lot. The bulk of his body disappeared into the rain. At that moment I was certain I'd just had a short conversation in the basement of the Saltillo University Hospital with Bobo Lafragua, the hero of the unfinished novel I'd attempted to write a couple of years before.

I wondered just when the hallucinations had started. If

there really were doctors fornicating among the corpses, or porn mags half hidden under waste bins in the restrooms. And I also wondered, for that matter, if Mexico had at any time declared war on the Axis powers. Or if, on the contrary, all this was nothing more than fever: "Mamá's probably infected me with her nosocomial bug and I'm burning up too." It was either that or the stress causing a psychotic break. I opted for the former: a psychotic break was a luxury I couldn't afford.

I ascended the stairs to male medical, and went into room 101. Everything was silent but for the torrent of rain falling on the window and the hum of the new infusion pump. Mamá was sleeping relatively peacefully. I looked at the clock: 5 a.m. I sat in the armchair and tried to convince myself I'd never left it: I'd only just that minute awoken. I went to the bathroom, banged my head against the wall a couple of times, looked at myself through my eyelashes, and touched my cheeks. Over and over again, I repeated "It's just fever." Convinced my mother had infected me, I gradually calmed down. But, just in case, I decided not to mention my visions to anyone.

GHOSTS IN LA HABANA

1

My mother is not my mother. My mother was music.

2

I remember being lifted up and set on a chair, and Marisela Acosta handing me a comb. I held it in front of my mouth as if it were a microphone and sang: “Fly, fly, little dove, fly, fly between the bullets.” The *corrido* was by Genaro Vázquez, a teacher and guerrilla who died (we now know he was killed) on February 2, 1972. I must have been very small when I sang that song. The guests applauded wildly.

But that, of course, is not my earliest memory.

3

Mamá had, as far as I know, just one platonic love. A guerrilla whom we knew only by his nickname (I guess it was, in fact, a code name): the Karate Teacher. Now that she's old, my story annoys her, and she says it isn't true, that she remembers the kid, but that I've made up all the rest. This would have been not long after my third birthday, so I may not be the most reliable source. But I didn't invent anything: I'm sure she cried when she heard of his death. That night, she didn't have the strength to go to work.

We saw him only once: we were with my godmother, Jesu, one Thursday in a pozole restaurant near the Mercado Central when we came across him with Jesu's younger brother, Kito. The Karate Teacher was very wiry, very serious, and very hairy. He talked nonstop in a low voice, with a lot of different words, a lot of saliva, and great intensity. I hated him from the start. Mamá, on the other hand, listened the whole afternoon with a dumb expression on her face. I threw myself onto the floor, scattered sand on the plate of avocados, and deliberately bit into a peppery radish so my face would go red and I'd cry. After each new stunt she would simply slap me on the bottom. When it was time to say good-bye, the Karate Teacher and Marisela clasped hands and looked into each other's eyes. This is, of course, my earliest memory: the anguish caused by a stranger stealing my only love.

I can't be sure how long afterward it was that Kito was arrested during a failed bank heist in Acapulco. Mamá, my godmother, and I visited him in jail, just around the corner from the house: at that time, we were living at No. 4, Callejón Benito Juárez, in the Aguas Blancas neighborhood, very near the Zona de Tolerancia. The three of them cried, and talked dirty through the bars. Then, in reply to a question from my mother, Kito said:

"Those ass-licking bastards in Ticuí applied the law of flight to the Karate Teacher."

I remember the phrase. I didn't learn what it meant until much later. What I do know is that night, Mamá locked herself in our room and got drunk listening to boleros. She says she didn't. Says I'm remembering it all wrong because I was just a kid. But who forgets the first time he sets foot in a jail?

4

Scared out of my skin, I thought about that, and other trivialities, the night my plane was descending into La Habana. I thought about them as a distraction, so as not to break into a cold sweat: in the pocket of my denim jacket was a piece of opium paste the size of a garlic clove. I was terrified that Fidel's children would throw me in the can for drug trafficking.

Someone—I can't even remember who—had given me that chunk of rock for my birthday. We took a couple of tokes off a small ceramic pipe, and then I stashed the rock in my desk. And completely forgot about it. Until, months later, while I was packing for the trip to Cuba (it was a business trip: I'd been contracted as part of a team planning a series of concerts and exhibitions of the work of Mexican artists) and looking for something else, there it was. It occurred to me it would be fun to sit by the sea and share the rock with some of my colleagues. I broke it in two, ground one half, dissolved the resulting powder in water (producing a sort of alcohol-free laudanum), and poured the solution into a small bottle of nasal spray with a built-in applicator so as to be able to sniff it directly from the container. I dropped the other half in the bottom of an open pack of Popular cigarettes and, putting both of these in the pocket of my jacket, set off for the airport.

I spent the whole flight sniffing liquid opium from the Afrin Lub bottle: between the naiads and the clouds, and people looking at me in compassion, what a lousy cold that poor guy has.

Shortly before we landed, the fear hit me: Cuban jails have an abysmal reputation, and it's well known that as Castro communism gets doddery, it's also becoming more conservative and puritanical . . . What had happened to the libertarian (and no doubt also stoned) guerrilla shadows my mother taught me to sing of, standing on a chair, with a comb as a microphone in my hand . . . ? Those jerks are right this minute dragging me away, hijacking me, good-bye blond Caribbean girls good-bye heaps of roast pork and suckling pig good-bye walks along the Malecón with your head like a bundle of lit matches from so much beauty good-bye *guaracha* good-bye . . . But at the same time I consoled myself: the positive side is that I'm so far off my ass I'll hardly notice one more kick in the butt . . . But tomorrow . . . I closed my eyes and pictured myself cleaning the excrement from a latrine embedded in the wall of some sort of cave, with my long, long curling locks and beard (me, with hardly a hair on my head), like the Count of Monte Cristo . . . Then, in the next scene, no: I managed to outwit the dogs and the grunts and I shot through customs like Bruce Willis in *12 Monkeys*, with that same peep-peep-off-the-hook-telephone music in the background while I was, in my narcoguerrilla mode, moving deeper into the tropical jungle: comrades, take a bit of this analgesic, down with the evil government, freedom, freedom, The Revolution Is the Opiate of the People . . . And in this way, I entertained myself so wholesomely with the djinns of my nervous system that I didn't even notice when the plane touched down.

5

By contrast, Mamá's earliest memory (because she told me about it: she tells me almost everything) is tender and repugnant. She must have been, like me, around three years old. She was looking through the gold threads in the speaker of a big Dutch Philips radio with two wooden dials. Someone—she doesn't know who; I suspect it was my grandfather Marcelino—had told her the music coming from the large, coffee-colored box was played by tiny little people who lived inside it. For all she stared and stared, Lupita couldn't make anyone out. Yet, suddenly, perhaps . . . But . . .

She felt herself being lifted up. Just like me when she transported me in her arms to set me in singer pose on a chair. Only she wasn't being held around the waist, but by her braids. Then she heard my grandmother's voice (and this is the first thing my mother remembers about her mother, so how was her life not going to be fucked up?):

"You Damned Wretch, how often do I have to tell you not to touch other people's things?"

And without an ounce of mercy, she was dragged out to the unpaved yard, where my child-mother thrashed around in the dirt, being kicked and slapped by what schmaltzy radio and television announcers describe as "the author of her days."

She was tortured almost daily. Because she wanted to go to school. Because she didn't want to go to school. Because one of her braids came loose. Because she didn't fetch the bread properly. Because she forgot to gather firewood. Because one of her little brothers (half brothers, in fact) cried somewhere near her. Because she was wearing a short skirt, her knees were dusty, her throat sore. But, in particular, that woman nearly whacked the life out of my mother for liking boleros.

My grandmother Juana fell in love with my grandfather Pedro at the age of fourteen, when they met at a dance. He and her brother—my great-uncle Juan—used to play pieces by Rafael Hernández with a band called Son Borincano. My great-uncle played guitar, and my grandfather the tres. It wasn't long before Pedro and Juana began having sexual relations, and my grandmother almost immediately became pregnant with my mother. Their respective families (neighbors and—until then—friends) made them get married. Apparently they lived together for a few months, until the fall, when Guadalupe was born. Grandmother Juana wasn't ready to be a mother. She panicked and ran away from the rickety house my grandfather Pedro, twenty years old and a truck driver, had managed to provide for her. Her flight lasted only a few days. Then, repentant or compelled by the women of her family, she tried to get the baby back. My grandfather refused to hand his daughter over, so my grandmother went to the police and accused him of kidnapping. Pedro was sent to prison. Juana got my mother back. When he was released, they say my grandmother wanted to make things right; have another go at marriage. But Pedro was deeply embittered. He left the city. Left music.

Still a teenager, at the age of seventeen and burdened with a two-year-old, Juana married a man ten years older than herself, a mechanic at the Casa Redonda whose only patrimony consisted of being plain, calm, and kindhearted.

“He’s got just one flaw,” said the matchmakers. “He drinks. But don’t worry, child, you’ll make him stop.”

Of course, she didn’t.

They say that in the mideighties, on her deathbed, eaten away by a cancer of the uterus—poetic justice—Juana asked her youngest daughter-in-law to look in her chest of drawers for a photograph hidden under the plywood at the back. It was a studio portrait taken on the day of her marriage to Pedro Acosta. She died holding it to her breast.

My grandmother never stopped loving her first husband. That’s why she detested the very existence of my mother and music.

It took Guadalupe years to fully understand this. However, something inside her recognized the pattern linking the blows to the bolero. She knew by intuition that singing or even listening to the radio in the house could be dangerous. She resigned herself to the times grandfather Marcelino, bottle of mezcal in hand, tuned in to hear Los Montejo on W Radio: behind the blue of your eyes is a radiant flowering of pearls. Or she would eavesdrop on the neighbors’ sets and, being careful not to move her lips, imitate the voice of Bienvenido Granda in her head while washing the dishes.

When she was nearly eight, in 1950, Guadalupe discovered one of the most furious wonders childhood offers: escape. She used any pretext—going to the bread store, throwing the dirty water onto the sidewalk, delivering a message to the woman next door—to run and hide in the park in the center of San Luis Potosí, relatively close to where the family lived. She knew no one would come looking for her: in the first place, they wouldn’t miss her; and second, because her flight would give Juana an excellent excuse to beat her, not just with the flat of her hand, but armed with a stick, a frying pan, or anything else within reach.

But just in case, Guadalupe took the precaution of climbing

one of the old trees and hiding among the foliage. She would stay there the whole day, putting up with the cold, the heat, hunger; especially hunger. She sang. Sang at the top of her lungs, as I saw her sing many times when she came home happy and drunk because she'd made good money in the brothel: in the sea is a palm tree with fronds reaching high in the sky where those who find no consolation go to cry poor little palm tree. Sometimes she sang solo, at others she accompanied the tunes on the station they tuned in to at the ice cream parlor by the gazebo in the park . . . She would sing until six or seven in the evening, when the sun went down. Then (she tells me, she tells me almost everything) she'd begin to feel a web of cramps knotting the soles of her feet. The sensation would creep to her ankles, up her calves, and, little by little, as the light dimmed, the web of cramps moved through her whole body until it became a thick, whitish, elastic lump in her throat. When she was convinced that lump was about to choke her, she could finally manage to cry. To spit the whole web out. She says what always used to set her off was a bolero that came on the radio of the ice cream parlor at sundown: "Sleepless from Love" by Trio Guayacán: I go back to sleep and I wake again.

When the song and the crying jag were done, calmer and surely cleansed of hate, Mamá would climb down from the tree and, on her way home, calculate—in the spirit of an abused wife or bad boxer—how to position her body to best absorb her mother's blows.

6

We exited the plane into a duty-free area, where I amused myself window-shopping: I didn't want to be arrested in front of the other members of our group. None of them were known to me personally, but I could identify them (and they me) by our uniform T-shirts; the organizers had given us ten each, and, according to the contract, we were supposed to wear them throughout our stay on the island, during working hours and transfers to and from the hotel.

My first evasive action was futile: all the members of the team were, just like me, looking around the well-stocked communist stores in the airport. Between the large shop windows full of rum and CDs and Cuban cigars was a tiny one with baseball merchandise: blue caps and shirts with a large *I* printed in Gothic; a small triangular banner with the inscription (also in Gothic lettering) "Industriales de La Habana." I decided to buy a baseball shirt and change out of my work uniform in the restrooms. At least that way I wouldn't embarrass my colleagues when they took me away. In the meantime, surrounded by tourists and police officers, I went on administering myself generous doses of liquid opium from the Afrin Lub bottle. Manic calm.

Two hours later, I managed to get through the identity screening, picked up my luggage, and joined the line leading to the exit. Directly in front of me was a very tall blond kid with impressive dreadlocks. We nodded to each other.

After half an hour, when the Rasta kid reached the door, the customs officer asked for his papers. He calmly studied them and eventually said:

"Come with me, please. Just a routine inspection."

The two of them disappeared through a mirrored door beside the exit. For a moment there was a solemn silence among those of us still waiting our turn: we all knew the "routine inspection" involved sticking two fingers into the Rasta kid's rectum to check for illegal substances.

By contrast, the guard who fell to me smiled without taking his eyes off my shirt. He hardly even glanced at my passport before returning it, saying:

"Three games to one, papi, three games to one. Blues on one side, Reds on the other. Thanks for choosing Industriales."

7

Marisela Acosta's ideology is—like that of any true citizen who has inhabited the twentieth century—a mystery.

She learned to read and write from my grandfather Marcelino. Then she did two years of elementary school but had to leave when my grandmother Juana needed her to help care for her younger brothers. What Marisela enjoyed most during her time at school were the numbers; even today she always has two or three notebooks with her, in which she records figures and arithmetical operations no one quite knows the meaning of.

At fourteen, she left home for good. She worked as a servant for a family from Guanajuato State, ultra-Catholics of the Cristero tradition. From there, I infer, came her passion for Saint Francis of Assisi (for years she never failed to make the pilgrimage to Real de Catorce on his feast day) and certain ingenuously aristocratic gestures and phrases:

"I'm an exquisite perfume wrapped in newspaper."

From there also came her racism and, given that she was from Indian stock, her self-loathing. The fathers of her offspring were all white and/or had foreign names. As boys we were advised:

"Marry a light-skinned girl. But make sure she's pretty. The species has to be improved."

She never lost contact with her stepfather; they were very fond of each other.

Marcelino Chávez took part in the railways movement at the end of the fifties, which makes me suspect he had a political background. It's likely that he was the source of Mamá's earliest Marxist ideas. What's more, Marisela initially arrived in Acapulco in the midsixties, and lived there—if intermittently—until 1977. That period included, on the one hand, the peak of imported U.S. frivolity, Acapulco rock, LSD, mansion whorehouses like La Huerta, old-fashioned porn, the first appearance of cocaine among the tourists, mirrored balls . . . But it was also the era in which Utopia had a shootout with the Wild West: the weekends of super-pure '68 teenagers, the first steps toward collective farming, the revolutionaries Lucio Cabañas and Genaro Vázquez, the Dirty War . . . All this was part of life in those days; but to perceive the process from a bacchanalian standpoint, as a woman, and from the tables of an Acapulco brothel, was—I like to imagine—like lapping up the cream of two worlds at once. Mamá would be making out with an ideologue of the teaching profession one night, and with the paramilitary captain who'd tortured him the next. That's why she thinks private property is a lie invented by exploiters and corrupt governments but, also, that—more recently—demonstrating in the street like Obrador's hoards shows a lack of respect and decorum in a country of civilized, educated people. That's why she believes Ernesto Guevara is the supreme hero of all time, but also that young people need to be taught with a firm hand, with principles, and even with blows.

She detests drugs.

"How is it possible that you, so intelligent in your own estimation, poison yourself with *This*?" she asked in the midnineties, when she found out about my cocaine addiction.

In my family, it's fine to utter any kind of curse (frigging, bastard, screw, idiot), but obscenities (prick, ass, fart, whoremonger) are prohibited. Although it's a bit late in the day for me to offer a clear explanation of the difference between the two categories, I can easily intuit which new words belong in one hemisphere and which in the other. The universal term my siblings and I employ to substitute impolite expressions is *This*.

When my elder brother gave me my first talk about sex, he never mentioned pricks or penises, clitorises or vaginas: it was all *This*, *That*, *The Thing Up There,* and *The End Bit of That*. To speak about her work (unless she was tipsy or furious) Mamá would say: *I do This*. For her, coke (C, White Lady, Fifi, the Devil's Dandruff, Soda, Snowflake) was *This*: prick, ass, fart, whoremonger. It took her a decade to forgive me.

We inherited *This* from an Acapulco cab driver: Praxedis Albarrán, better known as Pay. Pay was, for my mother, the nearest thing to a Pygmalion. He was about twenty years her senior and his love for her was unrequited. He presented her with her first copy of Carreño's *Manual*; he taught her (to some extent) table manners; got her used to going to the cinema once a week; made her read and comment on newspaper articles. He grimaced whenever she used a word incorrectly. He was a voracious reader, and each week he brought her one of the books people were crazy about in the last century: *The Third Eye*, *The Morning of the Magicians*, Curzio Malaparte's *The Skin*, *In Praise of Folly*, *The Three Sirens*, *In Cold Blood* . . . Mamá read them all, and later alternated them with books she chose herself (which eventually also became my reading material): Irma "The Tigress" Serrano's *A calzón amarrado*, soft-porn novellas autographed by Toni Friedman, copies of *Cosmopolitan*, *La casa que arde de noche* by Ricardo Garibay . . . Pay disappeared from the scene when a vaguely refined Marisela managed to seduce an extremely handsome drug trafficker: words beat looks, but gangsters beat anything that moves.

In the midseventies, two interconnected events fixed Mamá's ideological profile. One was (and for the record, this is not a pastiche of an episode from the life of Octavio Paz) a trip to the southeast of the country, the other, Marcelino Chávez's death.

By that time, my grandfather had become the neighborhood drunk. He lost his job for three reasons: the shame of having renounced militancy, the bitterness of years chewing over defeat, and, naturally, an excess of alcohol. He spent his life cadging drinks at the doors of cantinas. Not a week went by when someone didn't punch him. When Marisela heard her stepfather had taken to his bed, in the final stages of cirrhosis, she ran to his side. It was as well she did: neither my grandmother nor his biological children cared a fig about the old man's death throes. When Marcelino finally closed his eyes, Mamá took the filthy corpse, stinking of piss, to a room in the funeral parlor, stripped and washed it. She then dressed it again in the new suit she'd bought for his stay in the tomb.

The morning after the vigil, my uncle Gilberto said he wasn't willing to spend another night sleeping under the same roof as a whore, so my mother packed her bag and left. An "on the road" gang took her through the San Luis Potosí Huasteca to the port of Veracruz. She was drinking, she says (she tells me almost everything, with an honesty few children receive from their parents: she knows she's close to death and I'm her only apostle, the sole evangelist of her existence), any way it came: invited, out of her own pocket, ticketing in brothels, kissing men and lesbians, whipping up a Cuban *danzón*, at the wheel of a dented Volkswagen, getting off with strangers without being able to remember if she'd taken the pill or not . . .

Until one morning, while having a little hair of the dog in the café La Parroquia, crying ceaselessly behind her dark glasses, she heard someone at the next table say, "From the port of

Progreso, in the Yucatán, you can see something wonderful: the glimmer of the lights of La Habana across the sea."

Marisela inquired as to the shortest route, and immediately left for Progreso. She arrived the following day and, in the bus terminal, asked:

"Where's the place you can see the lights of La Habana from?"

They informed her. But one old woman warned:

"It isn't La Habana, child. Don't believe their stories. It's just the cruise liners."

Mamá didn't listen: she'd already got it all worked out.

So, she says (I no longer know if it's the fever or my mother speaking), she rented a small room and, as soon as it began to get dark, went to the piers farthest from the crowds and street-lights. There, in the dusk, she saw the flickering of a galaxy set in two folds of velvet. She said good-night to the valiant Fidel Castro, and sang, crying very quietly: black flowers of fate separate us without mercy . . .

Why is it that the lives of people who listen to boleros always sound so schmaltzy? Could it be that we only suffer the psychological predisposition to spy on those we know when they're crying, when they're in a mood that, in our heart of hearts, makes their presence possible: Lamento-Borincano fodder to nourish the Great Latin American (Tele)Novel(a), the signature tune of AM radio, the curse of Pedro Infante . . . ? Could it simply be that the bolero has a better narrative texture than comic music, than tough music, and therefore—to give an example—lachrymose tragic opera, *corridos*, the pins of Jocasta's dress are easier to swallow than, let's say, the comedy of Les Luthiers or Lautréamont . . . ? Or could it be an alibi? That we Latin Americans like melodrama because we are, Eurocentrically speaking, still mewling children at the breast, or impulsive adolescents? But then here in Mexico it's said euphemistically that people who cry still "have all their milk inside them": that is, are sexually potent . . .

This last point must refer to me. I prefer to imagine Mamá—drunk and sniveling—singing to the sham lights of La Habana than to see her as I do today: bald, silent, yellow, breathing with greater difficulty than a chick raffled off at a charity event. For over a week now, my mother has been, biochemically speaking, incapable of crying. The ideology of pain is the most fraudulent of all. It would be more honest to say that, since she fell ill with leukemia, my mother's political thought can be expressed only through a microscope.

8

On arrival in La Habana, I met up with the conceptual artist Bobo Lafragua, a sort of Andy Warhol (or maybe better, a provincial Willy Fadanelli) in his capacity for gathering around him a court of groupies, half-starved disciples, and girls so poor and so deeply conditioned that they take off their clothes every time someone pronounces (even referring to a brand of beer) the word *modelo*. My friend Lafragua (whose work was part of the artistic kit *a number of Mexican cultural institutions were bringing, free of charge, to the people of Cuba*: remittances sent by a brother mortified by historical guilt) had reached the port two days before me. He already had the city figured out.

We were being put up not too far from the airport, at the Hotel Comodoro in Miramar. As soon as I'd gotten out of the minibus, Bobo said, by way of greeting:

"We've had it up to the fucking back teeth with Habana Vieja. But don't worry, dude, it's real easy to get there. And I've worked out what to do if you haven't the time to go that far: the Russian Embassy is just a stone's throw away. No kidding, go see it, you're such a leftist dude you can record just how pharaonic those frigging idiots were. But if you go, make it during the day: at night, no way. After dark, the whole of Quinta's taken over by the most ass-hugging dresses in the Caribbean: sex on legs."

You could tell he'd already gotten through half a bottle of Stoli and—who knows—maybe as many as three or four lines. Putting an arm around my shoulder and pushing me gently toward the reception desk, he added:

"Tomorrow we're having dinner in the Barrio Chino, dude. And Thursday, we're going to the Casa de la Música in downtown La Habana to meet NG La Banda themselves. Then I'm gonna take you to a family-run restaurant hidden away in Almendares. I've heard they do wonderful lobster. But don't be downhearted, I've got plans for today too: go to your room and get dressed, I'm gonna show you something special."

Turning on his heels and addressing the tiny claque he'd already set up in the hotel (three little Mexican painters with contrite adolescent faces, who were looking at us warily from a comfortable leather sofa by the telephones in the lobby), one fist raised, he said:

"To the Diablito Tuntún, dudes."

The kids nodded, smiling in what looked like terror.

I've always been a fairly laid-back guy. With a generous dose of opium inside me, I'm a zombie.

I checked in, went up to my room, unpacked, and took a shower. Given the climate and my surroundings (the Comodoro is a hotel dating from the forties, low-rise and sprawling, three bluer-than-blue pools and four restaurants, a ballroom with an orchestra, and, facing the sea, two hundred rooms with wide terraced balconies furnished with tables and chairs that remind you of Hyman Roth's birthday party in *The Godfather II*), I chose a quasi-Yucatán outfit: linen pants, *guayabera*, and Reebok sneakers.

A short while later, I went back down to the lobby and waited with the three little painters for almost an hour. Then I phoned Bobo's room. Zilch. He must have fallen asleep.

(That's the only problem with my friend. He gets up at six

in the morning, and by nine is ready for his first screwdriver. At noon, he insists, "Let's go to a strip club!" But as soon as the sun sets, he's down for the count. A couple of years back, he had his gallbladder removed, which severely diminished his tolerance for artificial paradises. Sometimes I think he's the antithesis of a vampire.)

As we were already excited, and dressed for the street, the three little painters and I decided to continue with Bobo Lafragua's plans.

"Where are we going?"

"To the Diablito Tuntún."

"What's that?"

None of the kids knew: they'd arrived in La Habana just a few hours before me. So we asked a cab driver, who took us to the Casa de la Música in Miramar and pointed to an external stairway.

"Up there."

Before getting out of the cab, I administered a generous dose of opium from the Afrin Lub bottle. I realized I had only enough left for that night, and maybe the next.

I don't know about the others: I ascended the long staircase with the solemn sensation of walking in the alpargata-shod footsteps of Estrellita Rodríguez.

The moment we entered the room, the spell was broken. It was a discolored gallery, with a high, beamed ceiling and elegant but decrepit furnishings, like something from a rundown bordello: Turkish armchairs with the foam hanging out, tiny stools made of poor-quality pine and decorated with rusty gold gargoyles, artificial plants, and clapped-out—but Polar-beer-filled—iceboxes, groaning like gorillas . . . The music was playing softly, and some chairs were still up on the tiny circular tables. I checked my watch: it was just before eleven.

"No, compadre," said the guy at the entrance, reading my

thoughts. "The party doesn't get going here until 'round three, or four. If you want something before that, make your way downstairs. Sur Caribe are starting their set."

So we had to pay twice. I calculated that in just six or seven hours I'd already forked out all the CUCs I'd thought would last a weekend.

Ricardo Leyva was gently pounding the floorboards with "El Patatum" (if she's going to have it, let her have it, let her have it, look at the chorus I brought you), the three painters—indistinguishable in the bruised light of the Habana night, some kind of young masculine Graeae the object of whose single eye and only tooth was to see the rum disappear—ordered a bottle we finished off in a flash—the heat!—and it was easy to see, by the general lack of dancing skills, that nearly all the men there were foreigners, lots of Venezuelans playing at being communists with no sense of rhythm—forget it—and as for the Mexicans, better not say another word, we have a fascophile president and exceptionally timid syntax (except those who don't miss, at this point of the discourse, a period or semicolon) and we dance salsa with two left feet and our legs so wide apart we have all the appearance of Manuel Capetillo fighting bulls in black and white. The women, by contrast, were mostly natives of the island; they were as likely to quote Lenin to you in Russian as to put the *maquinita* into action without the pistons giving a groan, blam blam they had their souls in the feet softly brushing boards (give me more give me lots so my cylinder bursts), and it was difficult for a pair of greenhorns like me and the three Graeae of young Mexican painting to distinguish—given the good dancing and good posture—morals from politeness: between the loyal defenders of the party come to celebrate with the comrades visiting from the sister republic of Venezuela, and the easy girls whose thinking had been distorted by watching imperialist television (I don't care if you're *collectivist and friendly*: I'm Cuban, I'm of the People), and which, finally, were the licentious and openly negotiable hookers—or as Gente de Zona say: she-don't-give-her-salsa-to-me-she-gives-it-to-the-to-totality.

(May the Decent Comrades Committed to the Struggle forgive me, but when we're playing a beat we're all the same: up yours, Communist Party.)

Around three in the morning Ricardo Leyva and Sur Caribe finished off the show with a number many there were waiting for (I know because, when the brass section began the opening bars, the waiters passing around me smiled and gave me hearty slaps on the shoulder). "Longing for the Conga": Micaela went away and now there's nothing but tears, they say it's the conga that's tugging at her heartstrings, they say she's wanting what she don't have no more, and that's rolling out Chagó; a danceable blues to cast aspersions on the boat people. Criminal. As if the heroes of the nation had the right to brag about having expropriated our music, the dumbasses. But oh, oh, OOOH, that Shakespearean conga: suddenly we were all jumping. An incendiary percussion section, tamed from the street, wild beasts on the bonfire: some phony told me I was a rocker. We were the Walt Disney version of the May Day line dance in Revolution Square, the keep rolling on and stop at the corner, purely frivolous, whoring tourist trying to bargain for a piece of proletarian ass that will help him to experience, just for once, the erotic elevation—historical, Marxistleninist, and dialectical—of the masses. If you can't join the heroism, fuck it.

The music came to a halt.

We stayed on at the bar awhile longer, finishing off in two rounds a second bottle of Havana Club. Sometime after four, we went back up to the Diablito Tuntún. It was packed and sounded amazing, at full volume. Among the crowd we found a revived Bobo Lafragua.

"Why did you go out so early, you dumb dudes?" he asked, giving us his best smile.

Comrade Lafragua is notable for, among other things, his impeccable taste in clothes. He was wearing a white raw-silk shirt, comfortable Berrendo shoes, Montblanc shades, and a pair of cream-colored Dockers with a Ferriono belt. He'd tied back his shoulder-length, straggling, wavy hair with a silver clasp. He had a bottle of Stolichnaya in front of him, another of Famous Grouse, and several cans of Red Bull.

"You're just in time: I'm making kamikazes for our lady friends here," referring to the three hookers accompanying him.

We sat at his table. Without giving it a second thought, the three painters started downing the poisonous mixture Bobo was preparing: one part vodka, another of scotch, and two of Red Bull. I'd decided to stop: the alcohol was blocking the effects of the opium. Better to go on administering generous nasal streams of the drug.

El Diablito Tuntún must be the best "after" in La Habana.

I exaggerate: there are very many more. But they all come down to pretty much the same thing, sexual preference. The majority are underground dives, and what a pain to have to find a cab to go to Parque Lenin just before dawn to attend a gay rave, or how sordid to have to swig aguardiente from a bottle on the Malecón with twelve-year-old girls, or how expensive shelling out what they charge for a room in the Vedado to rub shoulders with ultrafamous reggaetoneros who seem to you to be yet more anonymous pretentious Cubans with gringo T-shirts and crazy Mexican-union-boss ideas, and how great it would be to move on to Marianao just to meet up again with the same mythical and common-or-garden scrubbers of the tropical dawn, with their scents, cloyingly identical to those of a strip joint in Paris or Reynosa, and after all that to end up fucking, drunker than a bartender's rag, fast and bad, in the same poky rooms with peeling walls in Centro Habana all the other tourists use, coming to the rhythm of the voice of the bad-tempered old woman in the room next door, slagging off you and the regime while secretly watching Telemundo.

El Diablito Tuntún is a duty-free whorestore where musicians hang out after the shows. Although prostitution is still illegal (which is why there are so many and such varied ways of practicing the trade in Cuba), in the Diablito the standards for judging legality are even more relaxed than in "legitimate" Habana clubs. The girls arrive in droves, wrecked from hours doing the rounds, but tougher than ever: greedy, fucked up, on the point of gagging from having sucked so many tiny, soft dicks. Sleepy, arrogant, grouchy (depending on how many CUCs they've made that night), raunchy. And though they would never confess it, with a desire to come, just once; horny as hell, a Santero of the Order would say. El Diablito Tuntún is a nightmare paradise where the music becomes unbearable and five or six girls dance around you, trying to get you into bed. You can't look a pretty woman in the eye here: they're more dangerous than jailbirds. If you look them in the eye, they undo your fly. It's the perfect place for a night on the town when you're a monogamous man, anaesthetized by opium and tortured by the fact that you're the son of a prostitute.

Before leaving Mexico, I spoke with Mónica: out of the blue, during a monster binge, I promised such solemn levels of fidelity that her hair must have stood on end. I confessed that my mother had worked as a prostitute for many years, and then informed her I was, for that reason, completely incapable of exchanging money for sex.

"So, no worries there," I concluded, without taking too much notice of the mixture of tenderness and horror in her eyes.

It occurred to me to tell Bobo Lafragua about this. Paraphrasing Silvio, I said:

"I'm happy, I'm a happy man, and I hope you'll forgive me if I don't go whoring with you."

Analytically, Bobo replied:

"Don't beat yourself up. The paradise of the Special Period is a thing of the past. Nowadays they're more expensive than a Vegas showgirl. Those European assholes—always ruining everything they touch—made them fashionable."

The conversation left me disconcerted: for the first time I was conscious of how menacing and oppressive the sexuality of a nation you admire and know nothing about can be.

That night, in El Diablito Tuntún, Lafragua, in his clumsy way, admitted I was right. Edging away from the girls he was supposedly getting drunk (in fact, they were more interested in closing a deal with the little Graeae painters), he whispered:

"Just when do you think these people fuck? They spend the whole day talking about sex in the streets, and at night they're drinking and negotiating sex in bars . . . Seems to me they never have time to fuck."

I wanted to respond with some platitude: all this is a ghost, a duty-free store; this isn't Cuba, we've never been to Cuba, I've never seen Cuba, it's a lie. I couldn't. The opium had elevated me to vaguely autistic beatitude. I thought: What are we doing here . . . ? I made an effort, and asked my friend that question.

"You," he replied, "almost nothing. You're already pumped up to your fucking eyeballs. Me, I'm waiting for a lady."

I must have been looking at him strangely, because he added:

"Not just any lady: I've got a special selection system going tonight."

The Graeae kids and the kamikaze girls stood up simultaneously from their third-rate pine chairs with rusty gold gargoyles. The kids felt for their wallets to leave a few CUCs on the table while the girls hung around their necks, touching their crotches, murmuring almost in unison:

"Well, if you're ready . . ."

It was a scene worthy of a sex factory, trading under the name of Plato's *Symposium*.

The three couples left. As different transactions were closed in various corners of the establishment, the crowd thinned. El Diablito Tuntún is a one-two-three-for-me-and-for-all-my-friends kind of place: it's full for no more than a couple of hours, and then everyone runs off like crazy to screw. For a few moments, Bobo Lafragua and I looked into each other's eyes so intently that two handsome mulatto guys came up to offer us their company. Bobo went on drinking his kamikazes. I snorted the last drops of my opium soup.

Out of sheer perversity, out of sheer self-loathing, out of pure idleness, I scanned the leftover girls of the night, trying to decide which one reminded me most of my mother. They all, of course, had something in common: they were slightly older than the average Habanero, and that was why they hadn't yet paired off. First, I discounted the blonds. Then a couple of dark-haired girls with big boobs. I also put to one side a black girl with an ugly cackle: Mamá always described herself as a very cool female during working hours. In the end, there wasn't much left: a girl with a shaved head, very fine features, and a slightly chubby face, sitting alone at the bar; a tall woman with long black hair whom I'd seen leaving with a client an hour earlier, and who had just that minute returned to the bar (very fresh); two gym types who must have been sisters, and who were whispering to each other two tables from ours . . .

"That one," said Bobo Lafragua, pointing to the tall woman with long black hair I'd looked at for the third time.

"Yes," I replied distractedly.

"Right: if you like her, I'll take her."

He stood and approached the woman.

That was when I understood his method of selection.

I didn't even manage to feel shocked: I was so drugged up, all I wanted was to muster enough energy to get up from my seat, go back down the stairs, and take a cab to the hotel and the rest of my opium. For a moment, I thought it would be polite to explain to Bobo that he'd gotten it wrong, tell him the woman didn't excite me in the least, it was just that her worn face had vaguely reminded me of my mother's old age. Explain that the harm he was intending to cause me wasn't kinky, but simply bitter, and I wasn't going to run to the hotel bathroom to masturbate, imagining how he was screwing the girl, but I was, the following afternoon, going to get up without a trace of jealousy or curiosity, without salacious questions or the desire to hear the details, feeling myself simply a conned whore: a sense of shame and desperation from which, in any case, I rarely manage to escape when I awake each day . . .

I didn't get that far.

I didn't say anything.

9

Ten years ago, I met a really beautiful girl. I'll call her Renata. She was (and I say this without boasting or with any desire to offend the feminist academics who scorn male Mexican writers, considering us incapable of including plain women in our erotic tales) the living image of Botticelli's Venus coming out from the water. Renata accepted me sexually on one condition: I could only fuck her anally. She said it was out of respect for her partner. I believe she enjoyed being penetrated that way but was embarrassed to request such a service from her lover. I, in contrast, was crazy about her and went along with her proposal. In the beginning, I suffered. She was small and narrow, my prick is thick and I'm uncircumcised; on a couple of occasions, there was blood. I was more inhibited then than I am now: due to the mockery and innuendos of the workingmen I grew up with, I was convinced the only people who did it from behind were soldiers, capitalist oppressors of the people, and whores.

Renata's rectum cured me, at least partially, of that atavism. Embedded in her buttocks, so desired by hundreds of television viewers (Renata did the weather forecast on a Monterrey channel), I'd say, "I love it." She was excited about the possibility of changing roles. She'd twist herself around and try to get her index finger between my buttocks. While I'd have liked that, I was never able to let her do it.

"Forget it, you fag," she'd say a while later, calmly staring at the ceiling.

I didn't respond.

For over two years we met fairly regularly in hotels, never going out together, and only rarely talking. Our friendship was purely tactile. I enjoyed those encounters in a perversely platonic way: rather than the orgasm, what seduced me was the secret pride of soiling my crotch with excretions of the ghost of Botticelli's retina. I'm not saying the sex wasn't fun. It was remote. A fiction.

The anus is a sign I haven't so far managed to decipher. In the abstract (as I learned much later in the poems of Luis Felipe Fabre, what makes this black flower so subversive is the status of the *abominable* imposed on it by the Eurocentric tradition: something unspeakable: a non-place) I've managed to idealize it. But, unlike any other zone of the body, I'm unable to address it directly: I can talk of it only in the third person. I don't sense it as a living beast, but as an animal I killed. I know this hunter-like perception should produce meaning in itself. Pleasure and possession need no outer splendor to be transcendent. I can verbalize it, but not feel it. And for that reason I admire in bisexuality a lost purity, a Neolithic spirit I lack. Judeo-Christianly speaking, I condemn the fact that the tastes and tremblings of eroticism don't culminate in a stubborn, irrational fantasy of reproduction. I'm a wannabe patriarch and a closet Opus Dei.

My ideological education and my childhood traumas have everything to do with this macho anguish about the anus. In the place I come from (but also, I guess, in any other place) the anus is the god Janus, the flower of the two faces of deceitful masculinity. When I was a teenager, I would regularly hear the men in my neighborhood saying the only true macho was the *macho calado*: the macho who knows what's on the other side of the track.

"A real macho," Don Carmelo would say, drunk as a skunk the night he'd been paid, "is the man who's been poked and didn't like it."

It was meant to be a joke. But Don Carmelo would always, at some point in his drunken binge, kiss Melitón, his eldest son, full on the mouth, slipping his tongue in too.

Don Carmelo was in the construction business. Melitón and I were his assistants. On certain Wednesday evenings, sweaty and completely beat after toiling over a job, we would attend a discussion group on People's Power that had been set up in the La Sierrita neighborhood, presided over by Méndez, a former militant in Proletarian Line, and Don Tereso, a retired railroad worker we all respected for his rigid pessimism: twice a week, he dined on a page of an ancient, leather-bound copy of the Mexican Constitution, wetting the mouthfuls of paper with swigs of water.

Proletariat Line was a Maoist movement that, from the mid-seventies to the early eighties, successfully infiltrated the unions of the Mexican steel industry. It was part of a much vaster mass project encompassing both the working classes and the rural sector, and whose last flowering was the Chiapas Zapatista movement of the nineties. It was, naturally, always grafted onto neoliberalism: hardly one of its leaders still alive today is anything other than a crappy PRIista.

I came into contact with the Mexican left through begging. When we were living in absolute poverty, my brother Saíd and I would sometimes go from door to door asking for anything people saw fit to give us: an old bedspread, a can of beans. At one house, the door was opened by a man dressed in the classic, fleece-lined denim jacket that was part of the uniform of the AHMSA foundry. The alms he gave us was Marta Harnecker's

The Basic Concepts of Historical Materialism, a horrendously untruthful book I continue to love with childlike passion. He said:

"Come back good 'n' early tomorrow. If you help my son clean the yard, I'll give you a few centavos and more books."

My indoctrination began that day. I am simply a self-conscious nerve in pain; in the afternoons I'd read slogans, old copies of *El Talache*, and Maoist or Marxist-Leninist texts in the worker's home. But at night, in the glow of the oil lamp in my rickety shack, desiring, beset by lust, I memorized Wilde's *Salome*.

Honest unionists are always going on about their assholes. They don't mention the orifice by name: they refer to it by the actions the boss, the strikebreaker, or the government-appointed union leader practices in that sewer of class consciousness. The two most common phrases in this dialogue are:

"He made me take it up the ass."

And:

"He made me take it up the ass but I shat on it."

The first is an apology. The second, an enigmatic consolation. In both cases, the one sticking it up is a son of a whore. The class of son of a whore I've never wanted to be.

Don Carmelo, for instance.

One time, Don Carmelo tried to cross a line with me just like he did with his son. It didn't work. Not because I was lucky, quite the reverse: it was because, by that time, I'd accumulated more than enough experience battling with the sexuality of very manly men. I'm sorry to speak badly of my mamá now that she's on her deathbed, but the truth is she didn't always take care of me the way she should have. And the problem with being the son of a whore is that, when you're young, many adults act as if the whore was you. My elder brother had to save me from being raped on at least three occasions before I finished elementary school. He explained the risks I'd have to run until I acquired the complexion and strength of an adult man, and he taught me how to defend myself from abuse. But to save his anus, a child has to be prepared to receive other, equally hard knocks. For example, the time—I was around nine—when someone dispatched me to the Red Cross hospital, down for the count after refusing to perform fellatio on him.

I like to think I was successful in safeguarding my asshole. Although maybe I'm fooling myself: maybe one time they made me take it up the ass and I've forgotten. They made me take it, but I shat on it: my mind blocked the event to guarantee a happy future for myself. Could be so: my mind is a second mother.

I woke to a particularly bleak morning hangover. The phone was ringing. It was near the end of my affair with Renata: the summer of 2002. I lifted the receiver, but didn't recognize the voice of the man who spoke.

"I'm an editor," he said without introducing himself. "I'm putting together a collection of *crónicas* about violence in Mexico for the Fondo de Cultura Económica. The title's going to be *The Red Book*. Remember? Great, right?"

"Of course." I said. "It was the collection of novellas with monkeys that Navaro published in the seventies: pure horror stories."

"No, no; no, no," the editor said in an annoyed tone from the other end of the line. "*The Red Book*, man: in homage to the great nineteenth-century author Vicente Riva Palacio."

"I've never read Vicente Riva Palacio."

"Ah," he said. "Right."

That was, for me, a sexually pleasurable time, but in terms of literature, depressing: I longed, on a daily basis, for any editor at all to call and share his bland geniality with me.

"We want to invite you"—I still had no idea who he was—"to write one of the pieces. We already have the big names on board: Monsiváis, Sergio García Rodríguez, Aguilar Camín . . . But we want to make room for young writers. You live in Monterrey, right?"

"In Saltillo."

"Yeah. You're in Monterrey . . ." He elongated the gaps between the syllables, like some well-intentioned J. J. Jameson trying to buy time while looking on his crowded desk for the folder at the bottom of the pile: hard-boiled Marvel comic aesthetic. "Ah, here it is! You can help us with the *crónica* about the murder of the railways union leader Román Guerra Montemayor."

"Of course I can," I replied, feeling first relief and then an icy deposit in the back of my neck.

I am (for a moment I was uncertain whether the editor on the other end of the line knew this in advance) the grandson of a Marxist alcoholic who betrayed the railways movement.

In the late fifties, Román Guerra Montemayor was a member of the Mexican Communist Party and president of the Monterrey branch of the Ferrocarriles Nacionales de México union. He was kidnapped from his home on August 27, 1959, and—according to Pilar Rodríguez, who survived the same raid—taken to the barracks of the 31st Army Battalion. There, he suffered a prolonged period of torture, until, on September 1 of the same year—the date of President Adolfo López Mateos's First Government Report—he died from the accumulated abuse. To continue his humiliation after death, and to fabricate a supposed line of investigation that would discredit the movement, the murderers—army personnel who had never had to undergo any form of punishment, as was historically the case, and still is, in this country—threw his body into a ditch alongside the Monterrey-Hidalgo highway. They had stuck a broom handle up his rectum and put lipstick on his mouth with the evil intention—doubly evil—of making the death look like a crime of passion between homosexuals.

Román Guerra Montemayor was assassinated at the age of twenty-six. That's what my mother told me. She in turn had gotten it from grandfather Marcelino, who had known the young union leader personally. At that time, my mother's stepfather was working as a locomotive mechanic in Monterrey. A few weeks after Román Guerra's body was discovered, Marcelino left the railways movement. He was promoted to chief mechanic and relocated to the repair workshops of the Casa Redonda—now a contemporary art museum—in San Luis Potosí, his home turf. The dirty side of this story has always weighed on my mother. Not in terms of my grandfather's dignity (dignity, according to my friend Carlos Valdés, is a petit bourgeois Utopia), but because of the pain the years following the movement caused him. He'd been a steady drinker since his youth. It was, however, those last fourteen years (1960 to 1974: from the age of forty-three to fifty-seven) that destroyed him. He drowned the ideological guilt in alcohol, and this brought with it humiliation, poverty, and, eventually, death.

I immediately accepted the commission to write Román's story. Not for the money. Nor was it (although I wish I could say otherwise) out of literary passion or loyalty to my biological or political origins. I did it out of lust: it was a good excuse for increasing the frequency of my visits to Monterrey to fornicate with Renata's anus.

I organized the preliminaries: making appointments to visit the city archives, the Fourth Military Zone, the offices of the newspaper *El Porvenir*, and Section 19 of the railways union. I also set aside time for a carnal session with my lover: 6:00 p.m. in a three-hour motel with porn and a Jacuzzi.

No one knew anything about Román Guerra. No one wanted to know anything. As if asking about one of the thousand corpses we owe to the PRI implied an insult to the Sweet Nation. As if the question mark had been classified as a federal crime. In the newspaper offices, I did manage to unearth the statements (very much after the event) of Pilar Rodríguez and Rosario Ibarra de Piedra, and an article containing an accusation made against four of the alleged murderers: Captain Bonifacio Álvarez, the assistant deputy judge Félix Estrada, and the union bosses Agustín Gómez and Alfonso Escalera.

At the union headquarters (beige walls, the smell of cheap maize, Olivetti typewriters, and black imitation-leather chairs, falling apart and with chewed gum stuck to the lower sections of the metal frame; Radio Éxitos: hits from the eighties) I was received by a bearded PRIist disguised as Tony Montana who, standing up and straightening his jacket to show off his gold bracelet, his gold Guadeloupian medallion, and the nickel-plated revolver at his waist, introduced himself as the secretary general.

"What a frigging stupid plan, my friend. Who the fuck remembers about that now?"

I explained: the aim of the *crónica* was precisely to release that injustice from its state of oblivion.

"Well, yes, my friend. But there are problems nowadays too. There are injustices. For example: those bastards in Section 23 in Saltillo go around unjustly, *unjustly*, making life fucking hell for my national secretary general, Don Victor Flores. And you come from Saltillo, right?"

I nodded.

"You see what I'm getting at . . . ?"

I nodded again.

He slapped his palm on the table.

"I'm glad we understand each other."

He was getting up to shake my hand in farewell when I blurted out:

"And what if I had credentials? As a journalist or researcher. Or had an official letter: something that proved to you my intentions are reasonable and exclusively academic?"

(*Academic* was the only word I considered might give rise to a little respect in a union leader; fool that I am.)

Halfway out of the chair, his hands on the table, after thinking it over for a moment, he spluttered:

"That's fine then. But make sure the top boss of the institution you work for signs it, not just some nobody. And you bring it to me before you talk to any of my union members, okay? Otherwise, I can't be held responsible."

I agreed. I thanked him servilely and left his office silently cursing, convinced I'd never return. I was almost out the doors of the building when a woman of about sixty caught up with me.

"Pssst. Young man."

I turned, and she slipped a scrap of paper into my hand.

"Look him up. The poor man's very ill, but maybe he'll see you. He knew Román well. He remembers it all clearly."

She walked away without giving me a chance to thank her.

I unfolded the paper. It read: Daniel Sánchez Lumbreras, followed by an address in the Ferrocarrilera neighborhood and a telephone number.

I waited two anxious weeks for the credentials: letterhead stationery, the signature of Consuelo Sáizar, who was at that time director of the Fondo de Cultura Económico. The document never arrived. The editor of *The Red Book* had forgotten about me; I'll never be one of the "great pens." And I wasn't doing much better myself: the *crónica* was beginning to feel like a drag, and the last sex session with Renata had left a lot to be desired. She kept saying:

"Fuck my ass. Tell me you like putting it in there. Tell me I've got a gorgeous ass."

But without conviction. I repeated her words in an identical monotone. I began to suspect Renata had found a new lover, someone who really did know how to hold a dialogue with that part of her body, as if it were a living animal and not a sock puppet.

I decided to make one last effort and, surreptitiously defying the union leader, phoned Daniel Sánchez Lumbreras to arrange a meeting.

"Yes, speaking," answered the tinny senile voice on the other end of the line. "What can I do for you?"

Feeling ill at ease due to a kind of diffuse anguish that was making me stammer, I tried to explain the project to him. He didn't interrupt, just politely limited himself to giving the odd grunt of approval while listening to my vague speech. When I'd finished, he replied, with a slight trembling in his voice:

"I don't know if this old man's memory is any use to you, sir. But I'm at your service."

A strange mixture: he seemed at once excited and skeptical. He agreed to see me the following Sunday. I contacted Renata to see if she was free too. She hedged, but eventually said yes, adding that we could only meet for an hour and a half: she was going to the movies with her boyfriend that night.

Daniel Sánchez lived in a clapboard house located in a rundown enclave of old Monterrey, two blocks from the tracks. His house looked not so much decrepit as moribund: it was clear it had been imported prefabricated from the United States decades before. The successive layers of oil-based paint covering the planks were flaking and peeling under the midday sun, giving the building the appearance of being covered in a decaying coat of litmus paper. Don Daniel was waiting for me on the porch, sitting on an austere, rusty metal chair. I guessed he was getting on for eighty. He was wearing faded steel-blue polyester pants and a white, almost transparent shirt, unbuttoned halfway down to his belly, revealing his completely white chest hair and the neck of a sleeveless cotton vest, also white. On his head was a Monterrey Sultanes cap.

"Are you the compradito?" he asked, getting to his feet with some difficulty and an obliging air. I nodded, and he added, "Would you like a coffee, compradito? I've got some Bustelo the whippersnappers send me from Florida. Good for the heat."

"Thank you kindly, Don Daniel," I said, just to confirm I was talking to the right person.

We went into the darkened house. All the curtains were drawn. It was almost impossible to cross the rooms, as they were cluttered with furniture, cardboard boxes full of oddments, and papers. In contrast, the kitchen, to the rear of the building, was bright: the door and window looking onto the small backyard were open, and the fittings consisted of nothing more than a circular Formica-topped aluminum table, an old white cupboard, a wooden chair, and an orange electric hot plate resting on fruit crates.

"Let me explain something," he said as he boiled water and put spoons of sugar into each of the two American ceramic mugs. "I was widowed ten years ago. I had two kids, one of each, but it's years and years since they went over to the other side. I've got a girlfriend, though I almost never see her 'cause so many ailments are enough to make you ashamed of being old. So all that's left to me in the world are my compraditos. Know who they are?"

I said I didn't.

"Anyone who comes here. They're almost all old men like me: when we can, we get together to play dominos on Thursdays. How's that sound?"

"It sounds good."

"Other compraditos," he continued, "are like you: red-blooded young guys. An' sometimes, like you, they come 'cause they want to know things from before." He emptied two generous spoons of Bustelo into the boiling water, switched off the hot plate, added a little cold water to the mixture, and, holding the pewter pan with a cloth, poured the coffee through a sieve into the two mugs with a surprisingly steady hand. "But that doesn't happen often. Usually it's pious people sent to us by that bastard of a priest, or relatives of relatives who come visiting to pay back a favor . . . Whatcha think about that?"

"Sounds good," I said again.

Sánchez Lumbreras smiled, showing me his perfect set of dentures.

"Hey, now. See how quickly you've started humoring me."

"No, no way," I replied nervously.

He shook his head, still smiling.

"So, you agree?"

He handed me one of the mugs.

"With what?"

"Well, to be my buddy."

"Of course I do."

We went back toward the porch.

"Grab one of those folding chairs, compradito," he said as we crossed what had once been the living room of his house, and now seemed more like a junk room organized any old how.

We settled ourselves on the porch, in the shade of the awning.

"No one has to tell me about Román Guerra Montemayor," he began. "I saw it. Such a red-faced little gringo, but he had balls."

After these preliminary declarations, he went on to tell me the story of his life: the rascally youth; his marriage and widowhood; the constant disappointment with his two children, until they converted to Martin Cruz Smith–style Chicano Protestantism; the kidding around at work; the minor bliss of retirement; the delicious eroticism afforded to well-groomed males who reach a patriarchal age . . . Curiously enough, the majority of his glorious anecdotes had nothing to do with the railways movement, or with his youth or middle age. Almost the whole story was set in the eighties and nineties: the era he clearly considered the happiest period of his life.

Around an hour and a half later, I tried to channel his ramblings.

"What about the railways movement? How did the strike start?"

His reply left me speechless:

"There are plenty of books about that, compradito. Didn't you know . . . ? I don't think you need to go pestering an old man to get information without giving something in return."

He continued his egocentric monologue for a couple of hours more; he spoke again and again of his unfailing marital fidelity, talked of the stream of girlfriends he'd had after being widowed (all kids: not one of them reached seventy), described his various illnesses in detail:

"One day, I stopped to take a piss, and this sort of coffee powder began to come out of my dick. Not powder: more like sludge. The wall separating my bladder from my intestines had perforated."

It was getting close to the time of my date with Renata.

"I have to go now, compradito. I've got an appointment."

"Well, be off with you then," said Daniel Sánchez Lumbreras with a frown, not looking me in the eyes.

Standing near the gate, I made one last effort:

"And there's nothing more you'd like to tell me about the death of Román . . . ? Nothing special you remember?"

His eyes clouded.

"Like I told you, compradito. There are books about that. What more can I say? Have you ever had a friend die?"

I nodded, recalling David Durand and Cuquín Jiménez Macías.

"Well, it's the same thing. It's just that for me they dirtied Ramón. Not the soldiers: good, worthy people like you, who insist on reviving his memory as an example of a union martyr. As far as I'm concerned, it'd have been better if his name had rotted next to his body by the side of the road, with a broom handle jammed up his ass."

It was getting late. I opened the gate, stepped onto the street. Behind me, not far away, I heard the sluggish brakes of a train sliding on the railway line that crosses the heart of Monterrey.

"What did you expect me to say, compradito?" said Daniel Sánchez Lumbreras, laboriously getting to his feet and finally looking me in the eyes. "That they fucked my friend . . . ? They fucked him. They made him take it up the ass. And then they made the rest of us take it up the ass too. Because we got cold feet. They got what they wanted: we were afraid. We were afraid and we said to hell with the movement. What did you expect me to say, compradito? That I'm about to turn seventy-six and I've had a happy life because some son of a bitch torturer gave me a lesson about Mexican justice, buggering the body of the purest man I've ever known . . . ? I'm telling you, compradito. I'm telling you."

"I'm very grateful to you, Don Daniel. Really," I said from the sidewalk. "But I have to go."

"You *well-read* people don't know the first thing," he answered with a look of weary mockery. "That's the only thing I agree with the oppressors about. You all believe the Revolution was a pure soul, like the Virgin of Guadalupe. Good luck to you, compradito."

I'm certain I've never before made such unpleasant love as I did that evening: I couldn't rid my skin of the sensation that my prick was a broom handle and Renata's ass Ramón Guerra Montemayor's body. I was raping her, not in the flesh, but in the spirit: I'd never been able to fornicate with her freely, uninhibitedly. I always saw her as the prostituted ghost of *niceness*. My attitude, as I discovered while ejaculating, was the most perfect example of ignorant, middle-class egoism: converting the sublime into the centerpiece of a table. Conversing with the irrational powers of beauty in the language of a weather forecast.

I never wrote the literary *crónica* about Ramón Guerra Montemayor.

I never again saw Renata, the weather-forecast girl: the spitting image of Venus coming out from the water.

10

Once, when we were children, at dinnertime, Mamá said out of the blue:

"If we ever have enough money to go and live in another country, I'd love us to go to La Habana. In Cuba the poor are happier than in any other place in the world."

It was the era when we were beginning to live like real people: 1980. Our house in Alacrán was acquiring its first flowerpots.

Soon afterward, when we were watching the opening ceremony of the Moscow Olympics on our first television set (we all adored Misha), Mamá noted thoughtfully:

"We could go to the USSR as well . . . But they say it's cold as hell there. And I wouldn't feel like going out to work at night."

From which it can be inferred that, in her thirties, my mother was a dreamy armchair communist, hated the cold, and had an anthropological intuition sharper than Fidel's: she knew revolutions also need prostitutes.

11

"I don't know what we have to reproach Cuba for," I said to Bobo Lafragua.

We were having a *negrón* in the Callejón de Hamel. It was before noon.

"This island stood at the very heart of our times," I went on. "Porn and failed revolutions, that's all the twentieth century was able to give the world."

People were starting to arrive.

A couple of days before, my friend had sought official permission to improvise a performance in Hamel "with the intention of offering an homage to the greatest exponent of colloquial language in Latin American poetry: the only poet capable of amalgamating, on a single page, negritude, revolutionary sentiment, and music." Enraptured, neither the censors nor the journalists who later covered the event asked the name of the poet in question: they all assumed it was Nicolás Guillén. I, who know my people, was aware from the start that Bobo was referring to Guillermo Cabrera Infante, then living in exile in London. That's the thing with Bobo: he always manages to make you feel perfectly at ease right before getting in a jab.

He responded, enumerating on his fingers:

"And music, and nerve, and colors, and a riot you can't just shoot down, and fornicating till you split in four: your Catholic and Aztec ancestors never fucked that way . . . Yeah: I don't know what we have to reproach Cuba for."

We sat in silence.

Then Bobo added:

"It's provocative, that idea of yours. Simplistic but provocative. I like it. I'm going to do a digital piece called *The Marriage of the Cuban Revolution and Porn*. A kitsch Photoshopped graphic showing a big mulatto woman in leather sucking my nipples, and Plaza de la Revolución in the background, in a composition taken from a William Blake print. It'll sell like hotcakes, you'll see. Especially among leftist imperialists."

The authorities arrived. An assistant approached my friend and indicated it was time to start. Bobo got to his feet and went inside the small bar to change. A few minutes later, he emerged dressed in an impeccable white dinner jacket, identical to Rick's in *Casablanca*. He was carrying a megaphone in one hand and a daiquiri in the other. The dark rings of several nights' partying gave him a sublime Bogartian air. It wasn't even lunchtime. Bobo raised his daiquiri in his left hand as if making a toast, and began to address the crowd through the megaphone:

"Showtime! *Señoras y señores*, ladies and gentlemen, welcome to the great, friendly, collective myth, *bienvenidos al gran mito colectivista y afable*, our socialist and tropical *Noche de los Tiempos*, our Shadows of Time . . . Prepare yourselves for what's coming: the autumn of the patriarch. Prepare yourselves to be offered hospitality by a nation of princes. To face its horrendous discourtesy, its venomous beauty. To soak up the last murmur of a Cuban beat between venerable Chinese residents and the subtle dispatchers of cocaine who follow you discreetly to the door of the bank, whispering, 'Mexico, Mexico.' Prepare yourselves to sit among more slender guests, being fattened for the kill with masses of pig meat. Prepare yourselves to be welcomed everywhere with all the show of respect a gangster can muster by use of his Visa card. Prepare yourselves to be segregated in a wooden outpost of the Coppelia ice cream parlor. Prepare yourselves to bribe. Prepare yourselves for the sea again. Prepare yourselves too for getting into the pool: the dental floss of a mulatta who'd pass as a virgin if this wasn't paradise. Prepare yourselves to be courted by the most fearsome harem of girls. Prepare yourselves for Elvis Manuel drumming up trade between radioactive beauties." At this point Bobo Lafragua sang: split my tuba in two, split my tuba in three, when I fuck you I'll give you, ay, three of sugar and two of coffee. And then he went on, in imitation of Lezama Lima: "Ah, you jump out a second floor window to get away from this reggaeton."

Then, with shameless gestures reminiscent of a good-natured, cockroachy gringo professor of sociology giving a lecture in an auditorium in some third world university, he paused for an instant to take a suck on his daiquiri. He raised the megaphone again and resumed his spiel:

"Prepare yourselves to be moved by the slogans of your youth: *Patria o Muerte Venceremos*, Homeland or Death. We Will Not Be Defeated. Imperialist ladies and gentlemen, we fear of you not / and the photos of George Bush / and Posada Carriles / with vampire canines / by a scandalized Statue of Liberty / in an unashamedly bourgeois spectacle. / Prepare yourselves / for the animal sound / of the 138 black flags."

Here, Bobo threw his megaphone to the ground, sucked on his straw again, and shouted at the top of his voice, moving in a way that reminded a frivolous militant like me of characters from an old classic Cuban cartoon:

"Prepare yourselves, ladies and gentlemen, *madams et monsieurs, señoras y señores*, for the great film of the future: *Ghosts in La Habana*."

And he emptied in a single gulp, without the help of the straw, the rest of his daiquiri, although all that ice clearly gave him a headache for the next few minutes.

Taking advantage of the audience's perplexity and confusion, Bobo came up to me, put an arm around my shoulder, and, loosening his bow tie and pushing me between the chairs toward the end of Hamel that leads onto the university steps, said:

"Let's go."

We were off like shot.

"We have to lie low for the rest of the day," he said, "and take full advantage of what's left to us of the island. 'Cause tomorrow at the latest, we're gonna be deported."

Bobo hunched over slightly and, playing air guitar, imitated the voice of chattering magpies, without diminishing the elegance imparted by his dinner jacket:

"When I left La Habana, God help me . . ."

On the university steps a couple of kids were playing pelota. We watched them for a while. Then we went down Infanta to Doña Yulla, where we ordered Polar beers and oyster cocktails in a glass. Not long afterward, Armando, one of the drivers from the provincial office of the Ministry of Culture, arrived. For a moment we thought he'd been sent to find us, but his manner was completely natural: he sat down beside us—his pockmarked face and honey-colored eyes almost identical to mine—and, without greeting us, told the waiter:

"Give me whatever these guys here are having. Two orders, just for me. To catch up with 'em."

He smiled, looking at us from the corner of his eyes.

Bobo took out his wallet and paid for our host's order in advance. They gave him the change in Cuban pesos, which were about as useful to us as toy money: no one accepted them anywhere.

"This is fucking awful, Armando," said Bobo. "I want something else."

Armando shrugged his shoulders.

"I'm off duty and I've got the van here. If you like, I'll take you to Regla or Santa María del Mar, or to the Zonas."

We spent the rest of the afternoon cruising around with him. First, we went on through the tunnel to the Zonas, but there was nothing there: tumbledown apartment blocks whose chaotic arrangement (F next to B; H next to M) only accentuated the nightmarish sensation the city was beginning to inspire in us. Then we went to Santa María del Mar: desert sands, locked restrooms, empty government warehouses. Bobo Lafragua took off his loafers and socks, rolled up his pants, and let the waves caress his feet.

"You see, Habaneros don't go to the beach on Tuesdays," apologized Armando. "Transportation isn't easy, and we're hard-working people. But you wouldn't believe how lively it is here on Sundays."

He made us walk to the end of the beach to show us what he described as "a historic site": a pair of natural pools in which the sea broke against the black rocks.

"This is where the rafts set out to sea during the Special Period. This is where I said farewell to half the people I love."

Bobo's buzz was starting to wear off, a situation that usually makes him crotchety. As he attempted to retie his dickie bow, he responded:

"Yeah, great, but don't worry: they're gonna put us on a plane and deport us. Know what I'd like now? I'd like to get my hair cut. Shorn. I'm gonna go all the way."

Armando cackled. He walked over to his Chinese van, drove it to where we were standing, gestured to us to get in, and drove off westward, to Habana Vieja. A few blocks before the Plaza de Armas, he said:

"Go straight on past the Casa de México. Two blocks after the Casa de Poesía, take a left. You'll find a barbershop the blacks use there."

He winked at us through the rearview mirror.

We all got out of the vehicle, and Armando said good-bye. He was holding a white paper package, with a label stamped very crudely in blue ink: it looked something like a two-pound packet of wheat flour. After hugging us both, he handed the packet to me.

"Tobacco. Not Cohiba or Montecristo, but very good: what we smoke. Take good care of it, Mexico, you've no idea what I had to do to get my hands on this without having it entered in my ration book. Smoke it right away, you won't be able to take it with you."

I put my hand in my pocket in search of my wallet.

"Come here, real careful. It's a present," he said with a smile, and then nodded toward Bobo Lafragua, who was already crossing the avenue to order a mojito at one of the stalls on the Malecón. "So you remember your brothers, the ghosts."

There was a hell of a row going on in the barbershop. The Santiago Reds had come from behind and were giving the Industriales a thrashing. The series was tied at three games each, and it was the evening of the decider (days later, I read in the press that Santiago had taken the championship). The barber and his assistant were cheering on the Blues. A policeman and two other clients came from Santiago, as does half of Habana, so the hullaballoo was going to last a while longer. Everyone inside the nine-by-twelve-foot fishbowl of the barbershop was shouting. They were so passionately absorbed that, instead of asking what they could do for us, or just cutting our hair, they ceded us the barber chairs and passed the aluminum jug from which they were taking turns drinking a robust, homemade cane sugar liquor.

After an hour or so, convinced we weren't going to be attended to, but gratefully tanked on the *aguardiente*, Bobo and I got up from the barber chairs and made for the door.

"Wait, Mexico," said the policeman. Everyone in Cuba knows you're Mexican as soon as they see your paunch. "Come over here, just tell me one thing: who are you rooting for?"

I'm an honest drug trafficker. In honor of the sacred opium stone (by then nothing but pure nostalgia for my respiratory tract) I was carrying with me in order to bring down the dictatorship of the Revolution, I said:

"Like there's a choice? Industriales."

The uproar broke out again. Bobo and I took advantage of the noise to sneak out the door and set off in the direction of Centro Habana. The sun was going down.

We wandered the streets for a while, lost in the darkness. The only things to be seen were stray dogs, very small, tame, and more than one with mange. From time to time we passed an open door with light inside: some kind of establishment. As with any other capitalist city, the Habana night has its stores. The difference isn't spiritual, but materialist and historical: the counters and shelves of Centro are—except for the very occasional bottle of unlabeled rum—empty. Walking along like that, evading sellers of pirated customs stamps, and following really hot, fat, black, braless women with our eyes, we came upon the junction of three streets with names that could easily pass for *I Ching* hexagrams, or symbols on an Aztec sacrificial altar: *Zanja*, *Cuchillo*, and *Rayo*; Grave, Knife, and Lightning. The Barrio Chino.

"Forget it," said Lafragua, "it's Chinatown."

We entered the narrow, winding alley of restaurants. Bobo

chose the most expensive-looking one. He straightened the lapels of his dinner jacket and, holding out a twenty-CUC bill to a diminutive hostess with Asian features and dress, said:

"We'd like the executive salon, please."

The hostess bowed and led us through the tightly packed tables, all crammed with customers, to the back of the room. We climbed the stairs and passed through one set of doors, then another. The executive salon occupied half the upper floor. It consisted of a dinner table with seating for eight or ten, a tiny balcony, and a small entertainment room equipped with a leather sofa and a twenty-four-inch flat-screen television.

Bobo Lafragua dove for the remote and switched on the TV. The only option offered on the screen was an interminable list of C-pop, edited for karaoke.

"I'll send a waiter with the menu at once," said the hostess in an angelic accent.

Bobo limited himself to asking, and then replying:

"Where's the mike? Ah, here it is."

The hostess left.

For a few minutes, the only thing to be heard in the room was the clinking of glasses coming from the first floor and the sickly-sweet pentatonic harmonies from the set. I went past the table and out onto the balcony overlooking the street. The lights of La Habana—from the scattered small houses, not the piers—were shining hopelessly. I remembered that anecdote my mother used to recount: from the port of Progreso, in the Yucatán, it's possible to see the lights of La Habana and say good-night to the valiant Fidel Castro. Dedicate a bolero to him: the black flowers of fate separate us without mercy.

Just at that moment, Bobo Lafragua let his beautiful bluesy voice flow through the room:

"Chi mu ke pe o ni yu, chi mu yang, o ni yu. Chi mu ke pe chi mu yang, ni mu ni mu num."

His invented lyric perfectly matched the televised melody. He stood up, still singing, and, microphone in hand, began imitating the conventionally stylized gestures of Emmanuel and Napoleón.

"Give it a rest, Bobo."

"Soo, too, ni-mu-yang. Soo, too, ni-mu-yang. Ka tu yan go wo."

From the inside pocket of his dinner jacket, he extracted a small comb. He threw it to me and I caught it. The symmetry between that invitation and my first melodic, revolutionary memory seemed incorruptible. I decided to play along. Using the comb as a microphone, clumsily copying the dance moves of the boy band Menudo, I sang:

"Soo, too, ni-mu-yang. Soo, too, ni-mu-yang, ka tu yan go wo, ka tu yan go wo."

The waiter who came to take our order was disconcerted. He attempted to reason with us, first in Spanish and then in Chinese. We didn't even turn to look at him: we were absorbed in trying to put together a new dance routine based on all too well known eighties steps.

"E-go-ne ma yu a-a, e-go-noh, go-noh-ke."

The manager was called. The racket (by then we were singing at the top of our lungs) attracted a number of clients. Some were laughing softly. Others looked at us with unconcealed disapproval. "What the heck," I thought. "They can't deport you twice from the same river."

They forcibly escorted us out of the restaurant. We couldn't stop laughing, dancing, singing as we descended the stairs and passed between the tightly packed clients on the first floor and continued along streets with steely-sharp names like *Zanja*, *Cuchillo*, and *Rayo*: Grave, Knife, and Lightning. And on beyond the Barrio Chino (Forget it: it's Chinatown), walking and dancing and running and dancing and zigzagging along the fine dividing line between Habana Vieja and Centro Habana, pedestrian precincts, avenues, and historical sites, Paseo del Prado, Floridita, Casa de la Música, the Granma in its museum, palm trees on the Malecón, the Hotel Nacional first above and then below us, El Gato Tuerto—the gas station where the gay kids hang out—the stretch of flags where little girls spy on the fat prey of Italian peccaries from their lipstick jungle, then turning again up the street toward Vedado to ask a gypsy cab driver friend, parked near the Yara movie theater, to please take us back to Miramar still laughing dancing and singing:

"O-ho-ho-he-la-fo ha no no ha no, ke-re-ke-ne-la-fo ha no no ha no, yu-ni-yu-e-la-fo ha no no ha no, haaa-no, haaaa-noooo . . ."

My mother isn't my mother: my mother was music.

FEVER (2)

. . . we know for certain that psychoanalysis, which believes it serves the reality principle, cannot abstract itself from the corresponding form of social domination, and so may unintentionally be at the service of the repressive system of that domination with its morality and prejudices. . . . In spite of all this, neurotic phantoms are not only regressive: in their core they are revolutionary, since they offer a substitute to an inhuman "reality."

Igor Alexander Caruso

It begins on a Monday.

First entry in the red notebook

It's a pack of lies. I'm repressed. I've never had anal sex. Bobo Lafragua only exists in my imagination. I speak several Chinese languages perfectly. No one will ever find a dive called El Diablito Tuntún in La Habana. I've never been to La Habana. That's a lie: I did go there once, but I never saw anything at all because I spent the nights in my hospital bed, suffering from a fever, dying, depressed and alone, connected to the black mask. The afternoons and mornings, I labored (in my habitual role of literary mercenary or prostitute) as the scribe of a sect presided over by Carlos Slim: a secret brotherhood of far-right Latin American businessmen who have been planning the future of the island after the death of Fidel.

That's a lie: miraculous Cuban medicine cured my mother of leukemia.

That's a lie:

So, from inside fever or psychosis, it's relatively valid to write an autobiographical novel in which fantasy has set up camp. What's important is not that the events are true: what's important is that the illness or madness is. You have no right to toy with other people's minds unless you're ready to sacrifice your own sanity.

Second entry in the red notebook

This is the way the world ends: not with a bang but with a whimper. What I'm attempting, of course, is morbid reflection, not the transcription of pain.

I wrote the story of my trip to La Habana based on notes I took during a Special Period of hallucinations. I managed, to the extent I was capable of, to combine three stylistic bodies:

1. the *true* entries, many of which were, unfortunately, unintelligible (I have the impression that what was written in the notebook was funny and tragic, in contrast to the coldness of my summary);

2. the perception of the febrile moment (or rather: what little of that perception I was able to preserve in my memory), something that obviously isn't mentioned in the original entries (no delirious person is so imbecilic as to lose the delicious thread of his madness by trying to describe it), and that I succeeded in reproducing through the fiction of opium;

3. and, of course, a vain, frivolous imperative: trying to write *well*, whatever that might mean.

I perceive the symptoms of my infection with love. I perceive the antibiotics with suicidal paranoia. I'm sorry: I can't pour that inner truth into the insignificant language of allopathic health.

I find the entries in my diary that make sense exceedingly boring:

> The day before yesterday my fever rose to 105. I was unconscious. Aurora and Cecilia, two nurses on the

night shift, put me in the shower. They gave me an intramuscular injection of a gram of ceftriaxone. They made me take 500 milligrams of Tylenol. They sent me home. For three days, I've been taking my medicine obediently. I'm halfway through. I feel better. Three more days before Dr. O. gives me the all clear.

What the hell does all that neatly groomed shit mean?

My performance consists of infecting myself with every possible germ and suffering fever until my pupils turn inward. Beyond the aesthetic experience the illness itself unleashes, there will be no other by-product than a logbook. I have to turn to the mechanisms of literature, despite the fact that many of my spectators consider it a dead language: otherwise the intervention would be just a tepid blot. I have to write so that what I think becomes more absurd and real. I have to lie so that what I do is not false. I don't intend to blackmail anyone with this project: I undertook it because I'm a Hartista.

"Hartista" is a concept that Bobo Lafragua and I coined to give some dignity to the most congruent creative function of our century: having had enough. We are the opium front men of a vulgarity that, a thousand years ago, was considered sublime.

I'm not trying to convince anyone there's art in this hartista-ness. I started it because it's the last resource left to me in my attempt to approach sensibility. I don't believe in the mirages of the new flesh, or in Moravec's arboreal intelligences, or in the information-religion of the couch potato: I don't believe in the Beyond the Screen. What I want is for someone to internally caress my old, blubbery, scarred flesh. If the world won't kiss me, let fever do it.

I don't have the diary referred to here. And I don't remember anything of what was written in it. Either I lost it during my convalescence or it never existed: it's another hallucination.

The story of the drift of these disjointed notes lies in the third and last entry in the red notebook in which I used to keep a record of the costs of my mother's hospitalization. It's the shortest, most enigmatic text, but also (not for you, but for me) the most revealing:

Third entry in the red notebook
Kill the southern dandy.

In the summer of 2007, a Coahuila Week was organized in La Habana. I attended the event as an organizer: at that time I was on the staff of the Coahuila Cultural Institute. I began feeling bad a couple of days before the trip back home. Nothing serious: a mild stomach bug. The problem is that, after flying from Cuba to Mexico City, I took another plane to Tijuana, where I was scheduled to teach a course. I worked in the Tijuana Cultural Center for a week. I bluffed: I have a dangerous ability for feigning health. It's not too complicated: if you're intoxicated most of the time, the people around you get used to reading your expression through a patina of chronic poor health. It goes without saying that I palliated the fever with alcohol. The kids in the workshop took me each night to a bar on Calle Sexto that's been there forever: the Southern Dandy. That's where Bobo Lafragua was born, and it's also part of the title of a novel I was never able to write: *Kill the Southern Dandy.*

Before returning to Saltillo, I was also supposed to pass through a book fair in Los Mochis. The people in charge of my travel arrangements gave me the cruelest of itineraries: I flew from Tijuana to Los Mochis at dawn, spent just one night there, and then, again at dawn, flew—for no clear reason—to Guadalajara. I waited three hours in the airport before finally boarding a flight to Monterrey, where Mónica was waiting to drive me home. After this protracted journey, I spent two weeks in the hospital: the stomach bug had become a serious infection.

The plot of my novel was meant to be simple: Bobo Lafragua, a Mexican conceptual artist, while traveling from La Habana to Tijuana, decides to stage a monumental piece of performance art in which he would purposely contract a fever in order to set down his deliria in writing. From the beginning, I conceived the character as an imaginary friend, a psychological Frankenstein, armed with the traits of almost all the men I love. The incidents involved would be pastiches of fragments of twentieth-century novels about Evil and illness; is it necessary to add that the major inspiration would be *The Magic Mountain* . . . ?

Some chapters would contain descriptions of Bobo Lafragua's pieces—narrating conceptual art is an emerging literary genre. One of my favorites was:

> In a room with white walls, measuring around five hundred fifty square feet, a transparent acrylic false ceiling has been installed at four and a half feet from the floor. To enter, you have to get down on all fours. On the acrylic ceiling stand mannequins: avatars of people walking on a transparent plate over your head. The floor is comfortable, with carpeting and cushions. There are even books in case you want to stretch out there and read. In a corner of the room, at ground level, a phrase is inscribed on the wall: "Anguish is the only true emotion."

The fever turned out to be more than I could handle: I don't have half of Bobo Lafragua's mettle. One day, I spent four hours alone with a sharp pang of pain that traveled from my middle ear to my molars. It moved with such precision I could almost feel every one of its steps throughout my whole body: dolorous particles. I buried my head in the pillow, but the pillow was an inferno. As soon as the fever abated, I decided to throw the character and his novel into the trash.

Some characters just won't go away. They wait patiently until you have a breakdown to come and collect what you owe them.

The initial stage of my mother's leukemia ran from October to December 2008. The second was in June of the following year. Although her first period of hospitalization was the longest and most painful, she managed to get through it with relative peace of mind: she wrote, stayed sober, was dignified. Her relapse, on the other hand, was not something she could deal with. Mónica was, by then, six months pregnant, and all my moral energy and fears were focused on my forthcoming paternity.

I'd begun to fall apart two days before the first meeting with Bobo Lafragua. In the morning, I bought a gram of cocaine, which I consumed completely in three trips to the visitors' restrooms in the U.H. It wasn't enough: at midday, I phoned the dealer again to ask him to bring me crack. I thought up an ingenious way to smoke it. As soon as dinner was brought around, I walked to a hardware store and bought a Yale padlock. When I went outside to smoke tobacco, I collected the ash in a bottle cap. Then I ran up to the room where Mamá was lying unconscious, locked myself in her bathroom, balanced the rock of coke on the keyhole of the padlock, sprinkled the ash on it, lit it, and inhaled the smoke through the open cylinder. It wasn't the perfect pipe, but it functioned. At some point, I remembered the ultrasound pictures of my future child and threw a half-gram rock into the toilet bowl. But the damage to my sanity had been done.

After our first conversation near the morgue, Bobo began

to come to me in screen mode. One night, I was killing time at my mother's feverside, scrolling through digital photos of the Berlin trip, when I noticed that in a picture where I'm standing under the belly of the Lego giraffe at the Sony Center, there was a small blue spot right where the stolen penis of the statue should have been. I zoomed in on the image to get a better look at the anomaly, and recognized in the pixels the face of Bobo with his mouth wide open, sticking out his tongue.

He spoke to me on the television. He was there behind the voice of a male nurse. I was soon noticing his features in the damp stains on the walls or in the folds or creases of the sheets. Four days after his first appearance, I went out to get some fresh air on the eastern courtyard. There, in the garden area, adorned with its deep-red and melon-colored mosaic, I stood looking at a squat, dried-out palm tree. And what do you think happened? For a few hours, I was transformed into a ghost, walking the streets of La Habana in the company of an imaginary friend in a dinner jacket. Mónica says that when Dr. O. came across me, I was trying to force open the metal door of the autopsy room, singing "Fuego" by Menudo, substituting the original lyric with syllables of an invented Chinese:

"O-ha-no-he-la-fo ha no no ha no, ke-re-ke-ne-la-fo ha no no ha no, yu-ni-yu-e-la-fo ha no no ha no, haaaa-no, haaaa-nooooo . . ."

Pretending to have regained my senses, I said to him:

"Apologies, doctor. The thing is my mother isn't my mother: my mother was music."

They sent me home provisioned with six ceftriaxone capsules and a pack of Risperdal.

The medicine relieved the pain, but not the dense putrefaction.

While I was recovering, I often dreamed I was in the square of gray tumuli opposite the Tiergarten in Berlin, and a man armed with a flamethrower was chasing me, chasing after all my friends, chasing the pregnant Mónica; he was trying to set us on fire. I would wake up in the backseat of a bus. We had arrived at our destination. All the passengers had alighted, except for one individual and me. I hurried to get off and, as I passed, recognized him: it was the man with the flamethrower; he was getting married that day and invited me to be his best man. We left the bus together. I was terrified; he was happy: well, it was his wedding day. There was an immense, circular, bare cement esplanade around the bus.

"Precisely," the man with the flamethrower repeated in a flat tone each time I realized I was still dreaming.

I don't know how many minutes, hours, days, dream layers I had to pass through to finally free myself from his fire.

Regaining your senses means your demons have returned to their place. They can't torment anyone any longer. Except you.

I was ordered to stay away from my mother for a month. I next saw her when she was discharged from the hospital.

"Let's get her a welcome-home present," suggested Mónica.

We went to Walmart and chose a beautiful black straw hat that, in addition to looking gorgeous on her, hid her bald scalp.

I begged Mónica to wait for me in the car by the exit ramp of the hospital: I wanted, for a moment, to expiate the sins of my scrawneebly soul.

(*Scrawneebly* is a word Mónica and I invented to refer to cowards: a mixture of scrawny and feeble. We stand facing each other, arms akimbo, in superhero pose, and recite in unison, "And did you really think I was scrawneebly?")

Mamá was waiting for me in her room. She was sitting on the sofa I used to sleep on. Her parchment-like skin seemed to me more beautiful than ever. She was wearing a laughable outfit: blue knee socks, black Crocs, pajama bottoms, and a red T-shirt. She'd put a towel over her head to cover the lumps and scars on her bare scalp. She was rickety. She stroked my cheeks with her two hands.

"How's my baby . . . ? You wouldn't believe how I cried when they wouldn't let me care for you, the way you care for me."

For the first time in many years, we kissed on the lips.

Diana had taken charge of all the red tape, so we didn't have to wait long: they brought a wheelchair (Lupita would have liked to walk out beside me, but protocol didn't allow it), lowered her into it, and we headed for the exit.

Mamá's face lit up when she saw Mónica by the door. She rubbed her almost full-term belly.

"Thanks for coming to fetch me in your car, Leonardo."

Mónica took our present from its bag. With childlike glee, Mamá threw off the towel, put on the hat, and hugged Mo again.

"Thank you, thank you so much, my dear. Have you got a mirror?"

We left the parking lot, happy.

Mamá never took that black hat off until September 10: the day she died.

III

LIFE ON EARTH

The most accomplished aeronauts of all are flies.

David Attenborough

When she was a child, Mónica wanted to be a scientist or a doctor. A woman in a white coat. As her mother is an anthropologist and her father a lawyer, it took her many years to realize she could be an astronomer or a marine biologist; she was only ever encouraged to take an interest in the humanities. I'm not complaining. Quite the opposite: I'm grateful to those people who skewed her vocation. If Mónica hadn't been an artist, it's unlikely we would have met. We're antipodean symbols: she's from the capital, and is descended from good Creole stock on both sides of the family, all bankrupt to a greater or lesser extent.

One of the treasures we have in our library is David Attenborough's *Life on Earth*, a paperback copy published by the Fondo Educativo Interamericano in 1981. The front cover has a photograph of what appears to be a titi monkey perching on some green spikes. I say "appears" because I don't know much about animals, and, what's more, the creature's face isn't visible: it's covered by a cut-out velvet-paper bat my sister-in-law Pau stuck there when she was in elementary school.

Mónica has read *Life on Earth* so many times she almost knows it by heart; that book was, along with her parents' divorce, one of those events that formed a division in her childhood.

On our first night living together in our new apartment, we made love on a mattress on the floor. We'd just gotten through a god-awful move: I traveled the eight hundred kilometers separating Saltillo from Mexico City by bus and, almost as soon as I'd gotten there, climbed into the car with Mónica and Maruca—our Irish wolfhound—to make the return journey, driving behind the truck with her belongings. I was wiped out, and euphoric. I wanted to share something special with my woman, a very intimate confession that would mark our wedding night with a metal heavier than that of rings. I didn't have the courage to tell her about my mamá's profession. Instead, I talked to her about David Durand's death. About the eviction. About my friend Adrián, who once accompanied me to Puerta Vallarta to meet my father. About how Saíd and I used to chase after the cardboard roof of our house when it blew away down the street.

When I finally shut up, Mónica said very softly, still lying on my chest:

"You're a beautiful sea cucumber."

I told her I didn't understand. She got up and, walking naked through the shadows, easily located Attenborough's book among a heap of volumes piled on the floor. She leafed through the pages for a moment until she found the one she was looking for. Then she leaned toward the large window of our new bedroom to capture a little illumination from the street lamps and read aloud:

> The sausage-like sea cucumbers that sprawl on sandy patches in the reef are also echinoderms, which lie neither face-up nor face-down, but on their sides. At one end is an opening called the anus, though this term is not completely appropriate for the animal uses it not only for excretion but for breathing as well, sucking water gently in over tubules inside the body. The mouth at the other end is surrounded by tube feet that have been enlarged into short tentacles. . . . If you pick up a sea cucumber, do so

> with care, for they have an extravagant way of defending themselves. They simply extrude their internal organs. A slow but unstoppable flood of sticky tubules pours out of the anus, fastening your fingers together in an adhesive tangle of threads. When an inquisitive fish or crab provokes them to such action, it finds itself struggling in a mesh of filaments while the sea cucumber slowly inches itself away on the tube feet that protrude from its underside. Over the next few weeks it will slowly grow itself a new set of entrails.

She closed the book, returned, and embraced me.

"Come on, cucumber. Don't be afraid of me. Tell me a happy memory now."

Adrián Contreras Briseño is my best friend. We haven't seen each other for twenty years. This is the only loss I regret when I think about my adolescence.

He recently called me. I don't know how he got the number. He asked after my mother's health. I told him she'd died. He replied sincerely:

"I'm real sorry, Favio." He doesn't know I'm not called that now. Then he added, "Pop's left us too."

I gave him my condolences, as sincere as his.

Don Gonzalo Contreras had been a man with a strange skill: he was able to injure a person without hurting him too much. Whenever one of the AHMSA foundry workers needed a few days paid leave for a trip, or to pick up another job to supplement his household income, he'd seek out Don Gonzalo, who would effect a calculated sprain or burn that, though minor, merited temporary disability leave. The union guys and reliable workers hated him for this.

Adrián and I talked for a couple of hours. We were perfectly comfortable: it was as if our last chat had taken place the day before. After catching up on the past two decades of each other's lives, we said good-bye with the same mocking, swaggering phrases we used when we were fourteen. I guess the next time we're together, when we're sixty or so, we'll go back to being children again. Friendship is one of the great mysteries of life on Earth.

Mónica and I often exchange a slightly macabre gesture of affection. One of us stretches out on the bed while the other shakes out the sheets over the one lying there, and lets them fall gently. It's an erotic, childish game: the sensation of lightness; the fantasy of floating. But it's also a bittersweet renewal of our vows: I am the one who will cover your face in that hour.

News comes from my siblings.

Diana is mad about chocolate and suffers daily from a youthful mistake: she ceded custody of her eldest daughter to her husband. They can see each other only on weekends.

Jorge has turned one of the bedrooms of his house in Yokohama (it's a small house) into a music room for his two sons and daughter. All three of them are named after European painters: Runó, Miró, and Moné. The room contains an upright piano, two guitars, and an electronic drum kit. He showed it to me on Skype.

Saíd was in serious trouble: the Zetas worked him over because one of his friends was late paying for a few grams of cocaine. He got off easy: they didn't beat him with planks etched with the letter *Z*, or shoot him. I gave him a little money (as much as I could) to see if it would help him sort out the situation.

Sometimes fraternity has no streets: just blind alleys. And a traffic cop standing in the blood saying, "Keep moving, keep moving, keep moving."

I don't know now if the country decided to go definitively down the drain after my mother's death, or if it was simply that Juan Carlos Bautista's prophecy was more literal and powerful than my mourning could bear: "Heads will rain down on Mexico."

Saltillo was no longer a peaceful town.

First someone knocked on the door of Armando Sánchez Quintanilla, the state director of libraries. The moment he opened up, he was shot at point-blank range. Then a *sicario* got mad when he found his wife with another man; he organized a shoot-out along the length of the Bulevar Venustiano. They say he took out a couple of agents before being brought down in a hail of bullets. Neither the press, the state, nor federal governments said a single word about the matter. Not long afterward, they executed a North American government official on Highway 57, near San Luis Potosí. The imperial machinery was set in motion with a vengeance, and, just days later, one of the culprits was apprehended in my native city. That put us in the thick of it.

Last Friday, Leonardo and Mónica were driving back from the supermarket along one of the main avenues when a police officer stepped out in front of the car and, pistol in hand, made them turn off onto a side street. They could hear gunshots in the distance. As they were coming up from an underpass, Mónica saw two military tanks on the highway above her with machine guns at the ready, pointed toward the flow of traffic;

that is to say, toward her and our baby. After that, there were three days of gunfire. Federal agents and cartel *sicarios* died in a confrontation on the Luis Echeverría beltway around the La Torrelit exit. At the gates of a kindergarten, a stray bullet killed a woman who was picking up her nephew. We took our EcoSport in for its six-thousand-mile service and then weren't able to collect it: a nonexistent—according to Governor Jorge Torres—narcoblockade got in the way. There's talk of grenades being thrown at the Sixth Military Zone, civilians dead and wounded, talk of *narcomantas* bearing messages or threats from the cartels. And again: neither the press nor the government issuing any information, and this despite the existence of photos, videos, and dozens of witnesses. If you want to know what's going on you have to follow along on Twitter. And worse still: in a fit of unmitigated naïveté, the governor declared that a fine or imprisonment would be imposed on "anyone spreading rumors."

(I hope when they come to arrest me, Jorge Torres will understand that what I'm writing is a work of fiction: Saltillo is, as he describes it in his stupid stuttering speeches, a safe place.)

We're always hearing about what a headache the frontier is for the United States because of the drug trafficking. No one mentions how dangerous the United States frontier is for Mexicans because of the trafficking of arms. And, when the subject does come up, the neighboring attorney general points out: "It's not the same thing: the drugs are of illegal *origin*, the arms aren't." As if there was a majestic logic in considering that in comparison with the destructive power of a marijuana joint, an AK-47 is just a child's toy.

Heads will rain down on Mexico.

On the return leg of our second trip to Berlin, we had a long, tedious stopover in Heathrow airport. We walked from one end of the terminal to the other. Mónica's feet were badly swollen and the fetus Leonardo was kicking away in her belly, but sitting down would have been worse: we were too anxious to get home. In a bookstore, Mónica found a small section of popular science books. She bought two: *Elephants on Acid* by Alex Boese and Frank Ryan's *Virolution*. Boese's book (which we read together) is a quasi-Rabelaisian satire of science: it tells, by means of episodes written with virtuous ill intent, of some of the most bizarre, comical, cruel, and absurd scientific experiments ever conducted.

Ryan's book contains harder science and pays homage to an old philosophical conceit: the human condition is a disease. Man is an abomination of nature. If I remember correctly, Lichtenberg summed up this conviction in one of his aphorisms. The twentieth century simply identified and popularized this point of view, exemplified by Agent Smith's monologue in *The Matrix*.

"I'd like to share a revelation that I've had during my time here. It came to me when I tried to classify your species and I realized that you're not actually mammals. Every mammal on this planet instinctively develops a natural equilibrium with the surrounding environment but you humans do not. You move to an area and you multiply and multiply until every natural resource is consumed, and the only way you can survive is to spread to another area. There is another organism on this planet that follows the same pattern. Do you know what it is . . . ? A virus. Human beings are a disease. A cancer."

The difference between the view of the Zombie in the software and Ryan's text is that the latter is based on something more than a moralistoid metaphor:

> When, in 2001, the human genome was sequenced for the first time, we were confronted by several surprises. One was the sheer lack of genes: where we had anticipated perhaps 100,000 there were actually as few as 20,000. A bigger surprise came from analysis of the genetic sequences, which revealed that these genes made up a mere 1.5 per cent of the genome. This is dwarfed by DNA deriving from viruses, which amounts to roughly 9 per cent. On top of that, huge chunks of the genome are made up of mysterious virus-like entities called *retrotransposons,* pieces of selfish DNA that appear to serve no function other than to make copies of themselves. These account for no less than 34 per cent of our genome. All in all, the virus-like components of the human genome amount to almost half of our DNA.

It's called "symbiogenesis" and is, so far, an audacious footnote to Charles Darwin's theory of the evolution of the species. The implicit notion is that retroviruses (AIDS, for example) and certain forms of cancer or leukemia are, rather than an Evil, simple evolutionary processes; not human death, but viral life: adaptation of the fittest. Nothing is going to stop them. We aren't going to bequeath the planet to our machines, but to the microscopic undead that live writing the apocalypse of our genetic code. My mother was never my mother. My mother is a walking virus.

Mónica has a brother and a sister: Diego and Paulina. Diego is an architect and Pau a lawyer. Diego is married to Orli, who does market research for an advertising agency. Pau is married to César, a financier who plays soccer and goes to wine tastings in his free time. Diego and Orli have two children: Gal and Yan. Pau and César have one daughter: Regina. I've only met Joaquín, my father-in-law, four or five times. By contrast, with my mother-in-law, Lourdes, I've been able to form a visceral relationship: a love that goes beyond etiquette. They all live in Mexico City. From time to time we organize trips to the beach together, or they come to spend Christmas with us in Saltillo.

That's weird: carving the turkey, whacking the piñata, counting candles in the company of close strangers . . . It's weird. Not just for me, but for anyone. There's no way to be human, sufficiently human, without at the same time feeling an urge something like that of the sea cucumber: the desire to escape by hurling your guts at your neighbor. If we manage to prevent this from happening in family situations, it is due to an impulse more radical than fear: love. Fear acts like a mammal. Love, on the other hand, acts like a virus: it injects itself into something; it reproduces without thought; it egotistically takes possession of its host, without consideration for the species, taxonomy, or health; it is symbiotic. Love is a powerful virus.

Leonardo was born on September 25, 2009: two weeks after my mamá's death. They only just missed meeting. It makes me shudder a little to think of how chance placed these two notches on my life. A touch of superstition must have filtered into my DNA after so many centuries of ritual.

He didn't want to come out. We had to send in a squadron of doctors to fetch him. We spent over twelve hours walking the hospital corridors, with Mónica hooked up to a large bottle of oxytocin, before the task of giving birth began. And even then, zilch. He had to be removed by caesarean.

He's a fair-skinned, rosy-cheeked child with light-brown hair and his mother's deep-blue eyes. When I'm holding him in my arms, and she isn't there, I get edgy: in my autoracist fantasy, I imagine all the well-bred people who must be looking at me suspiciously, thinking I've stolen him. If she'd seen him, Mamá would have thought I'd followed her precept of "improving the species" down to the last detail.

When they first put him in my arms, I clearly heard the most depraved layer of my bestial mantle rip. It was something like (multiplied by ten thousand, by a hundred thousand, by a million) the time when, swimming in a subterranean river, almost running out of air, I made an extra push to dive down to touch the veil of warm, turbulent water flowing very slowly in the opposite direction, at the bottom of a cave.

For years I wondered which of us was the ghost: my father or me. He was also the victim of a civil-register practical joke. As the child of unmarried parents, he was given the two surnames of my grandmother Thelma. His name was Gilberto Herbert Gutiérrez. A short time after my birth, he met his progenitor. As my grandfather (I've never known his first name) agreed to recognize him, my father then began to be called Gilberto Membreño Herbert.

When I was twelve, I said to Marisela:

"It's like my father's got two faces."

She explained that the bearded man who used to buy me toys when I was a baby wasn't my father, but Saíd's. We hadn't seen Gilberto Membreño since I was four. The reason for this was that he loved me violently: every time we were together, he tried to kidnap me. He wanted to change my surname. He thought a prostitute was incapable of being a good mother to me. Once, desperate to separate me from her, he smashed her into the dashboard of an automobile. Mamá and I jumped out and ran. From the sidewalk, I said to him, "When I grow up I'm gonna get you, motherfucker."

I next saw him when I was fifteen. He paid for a trip to the beach for me and Adrián, my best friend. We met up in Puerto Vallarta. I hadn't read the *Odyssey* yet, but I'd just finished *Pedro Páramo*. The voice of Juan Preciado's mother echoed in my head:

"Don't ask him for anything. Demand what's ours. What he should have given me but never did . . . The way he abandoned us, my boy, make him pay for that."

It was a disaster. He had to work ten hours a day (as the manager of the hotel we stayed in) and was dating a dumb gringa whose ditsiness ruined any attempt at melodrama. I couldn't get over the shock of seeing that his face was different from the father of my childhood memories. And then, worst of all, there were the Guadalajara girls: Adrián and I would have given anything to lose our virginity in the arms of one of those convent school bikinied babes.

The next time I saw him was eleven years later, when he asked me to come to my grandmother Thelma's house in Atlixco, Puebla State. He wanted to introduce me to Teto, my younger half brother. I was twenty-six and I think Teto was eighteen. We hit it off immediately; I guess we still had some aftertaste of that elemental bond Rousseau talks about. Gilberto Membreño was happy to have a drink in the company of his two male children for the first time. That was when I became aware of the extent of his alcohol dependence: he religiously drank a whole bottle of whiskey or tequila a day. From time to time, he went on the wagon. To achieve this, he had to spend several hours hooked up to a bottle of saline solution.

One night, we all went out on the town, and walked back to my grandmother's just before dawn. Hugging Teto and me, Papá said:

"Ay, my boys. We really have drunk ourselves sober."

I wanted to kill him. I wanted to kiss him on the lips.

We met again in 1999. I'd seduced my secretary's daughter. Her mother found out and told the girl to stop seeing me. Ana Sol ran away from home with a small suitcase and came to live in my attic. I got depressed: Lupita (my ex-mother-in-law shares my mamá's name) had been more than good to me, and I'd betrayed her. She knew about my cocaine addiction, which made things worse. I felt I was in love, but also poisoned by confusion and guilt.

I don't know why I rang him. I explained the situation, without omitting the smallest detail. For once in his life, my father behaved like a father.

"You need to kick the drugs and take a step back, son. Bring your woman here to Cancún. I'll cover it."

Ana Sol and I arrived at my papá's house three days before Teto. What I didn't know was that Gilberto Membreño was taking his leave of the Maya Riviera, where he'd spent the nineties. He'd just married Marta (who was then, like me, twenty-eight) and they were planning to settle down together in Mexico City, where they would open a travel agency.

The day after our arrival, the new owner of Gilberto's house came to collect the keys. Everything was already packed up. Marta, Papá, Ana Sol, and I moved into the Fiesta Americana, where he'd managed to get courtesy rooms. Teto met up with us there. After that, always for free thanks to his industry contacts, we spent nights in other hotels: Caesar's Park, the Meliá Turquesa, the Meliá Cancún . . . We continued this haphazard existence until the night a new plan emerged: rather than putting Papá's cars on the back of a trailer bound for the capital, and then making the journey by plane ourselves, we decided to go the whole way overland, driving both cars, stopping wherever an industry acquaintance could give us free lodging. The cars were a red Ford Fairmont dating from the eighties, and the beautifully maintained white 1965 Mustang Señor Membreño had named Prince.

The initial idea was for Teto and me to do the driving: that way my father could drink at his leisure. I explained I couldn't drive. He was shocked. In the end, Ana Sol and Teto took turns at the wheel of the Fairmont, and Marta and Gilberto drove the

Mustang. For a few days, Ana Sol had a crush on my younger brother: she realized she'd gotten the short straw when she ended up with the stocky, ugly old kid of the family. It passed.

We stopped in Mérida, Telchac, and Campeche. In Villahermosa, the Fairmont packed up for four days: days during which we relieved the boredom with free drinks from the minibar. We made a brief halt in Veracruz. Finally, after nine days on the road, we got to my grandmother's house in Atlixco, where we said our good-byes. The whole way, Gilberto Membreño was a patient, understanding, affectionate father. In my grandmother's house, he took me to her bedroom (no man was allowed to enter that room) and showed me a picture hanging over the dressing table: a horrible portrait of me that seemed to have been airbrushed. My hair is long and I'm wearing a white shirt with the number seven on the chest. It was dated 1974.

I didn't tell him (this is the first time I've acknowledged it), but I decided right then never to see him again. Why ruin such a perfect memory, such a sweet journey?

I returned to Saltillo. I stopped doing cocaine. I married Ana Sol. We got divorced. I started doing cocaine again. I lived with Anabel. Then with Lauréline. I tried to kill myself. I met Mónica. We had a son. My mother died. More than ten years went by.

Seven months after the death of Guadalupe Chávez, I received an invitation to a literary conference in Acapulco. I hesitated: Could I battle so soon with the ghost of Marisela Acosta walking the streets of that city where she'd been so happy, a ghost wearing an obscene pair of shorts that covered only half her ass? It had been twenty years since I'd set foot in the port in which I was born.

I accepted the invitation.

I knew, from sporadic telephone messages, that my father's business had gone bust, he'd divorced Marta, and had, for some years, been living with Teto. I asked myself whether it might be a good idea to call and invite them to dinner. And I answered: "Tomorrow" (only to answer the same the next day).

They put me up in an old, very lovely hotel with a view of La Quebrada. As soon as I arrived (it would have been four or five in the afternoon), I bumped into Marcelo Uribe and Christopher Domínguez in the lobby. They appeared to have agreed to blend into the architecture and decor of their surroundings: Marcelo was wearing a panama hat and Christopher a dark-gray Stetson. I checked in, left my suitcase in my room, and went down to the outdoor restaurant. There were too many writers: Jorge Esquinca, Luis Armenta, Ernesto Lumbreras, Citla Guerrero, Jere Marquines, Hernán Bravo Varela, Alan Mills, Tere Avedoy, and perhaps fifty more I can't remember now. The atmosphere was oppressive. A few hours later, there was a rainstorm. The torches of the divers throwing themselves from the rocks went out long before falling into the choppy sea.

One curious incident occurred: I was introduced to Mario Bellatin, and when we touched, a thunderclap sounded from very close by. Mario smiled and, hugging me, said:

"Settled, right?"

I was vain enough to believe he was referring to a literary bond between us. I now know that Mario Bellatin is an incarnation of Mephistopheles, and was simply giving me advance warning of the telephone call I was about to receive.

At midnight, I invited Alan Mills and a few of the youngest guys to my room to continue drinking. Fifteen minutes later the phone rang. It was Mónica.

"Oh, Julián . . . You're not going to believe this."

"What?"

"I hate to have to . . ."

"What?"

"Your brother Teto called. Your father's dead. He had a massive heart attack."

I asked my friends to leave me alone for a while. I didn't know what to do. After all, I'd secretly buried my old man ten years before. A muffled inner voice (the voice of the cynical, abusive, Hartista son of a bitch that I am) said: "This is good material for the ending of your novel." I cursed Paul Auster and his poetic feeling for chance.

Mónica says that before ringing off, I repeated the same phrase several times:

"I'm an orphan."

I believe I was referring to an anguish springing from a biological fact, not any form of spiritual sorrow. But anguish is the only true emotion.

I plucked up my courage and called Teto's cell phone. He must have been surprised when he saw the area code because he asked:

"How did you get here so fast?"

I didn't know how to answer.

The funeral service was to be the following day: Papá had gone to Atlixco to visit my grandmother, and that's where the heart attack struck him down. When we spoke, Teto was on the road, on his way to collect the body. We agreed to talk again in the morning. I offered him my condolences and hung up.

The truly tragic aspect of all this was struggling with my affection for my father: there were *too many* writers at that literary conference. By breakfast, they'd all heard of my misfortune. I fulfilled my duties: in the morning I went to the conference room and delivered my lecture. The rest of the time, I was pretty much in hiding. Even so, more condolences were aimed at me than my body could bear: knife blows to the liver. Poor people. How were they to know . . . ? I spent the whole afternoon throwing up.

At midday, I telephoned Teto's wife. She gave me the address of the funeral parlor. The show would begin at five. I put off my departure until ten that night and, in the interim, watched a couple of movies and went out onto the balcony of my room to view the spectacle of La Quebrada: half-naked scrawneeblies throwing themselves, one after the other, headfirst onto the rocks. Acapulco should be designated a federal crime.

I finally left the hotel. Got in a cab. Gave the driver the address of the funeral parlor. It wasn't far: on Cuauhtémoc, just before the junction with what had once for me been the canal street and is now a wide avenue with several underpasses. The glass door wasn't very wide. The street—like all streets in Acapulco—was filled with trash. There were two chapels inside the establishment. I immediately knew which was my father's: I recognized Teto, in suit and tie, squatting down, his head and hands resting in the lap of an older seated woman who must have been Señora Abarca: his mother. A woman in her thirties was stroking my brother's hair. I don't know if she was his wife or my half sister Betty: I'd never met either of them. There were enough mourners for me to pass unnoticed by the door for a minute. As long as was needed to mentally repeat the question that had been eating away at me since I was twelve: Which of us was the ghost, my father or me . . . ?

The funeral scene said it all. Without either greeting or saying farewell to Gilberto's body, I turned and walked away from the home of the Membreño Abarcas, a mansion I had held under a spell for almost forty years.

There's an orchard next to my house: twenty-two acres of walnut, apple, quince, privet, and poplar trees. Leonardo and I go there every day. Sometimes for a couple of hours. Sometimes only for a minute or two. It depends on him. If he's in the mood, we walk to the small tumbledown house, turn toward El Morillo, cut through the old carpentry workshop to say hello to the cows, go down and up the banks of the gully, give an apple to Hernán's horse, and stop for a while at the large yellow door at the back to wait for a train to pass. If he isn't in the mood, we sit among the dry leaves at the entrance to Martha's house and eat ants.

Whenever we're there, I think of Marisela Acosta: I can't escape the fact that the most famous brothel she worked in was called La Huerta, The Orchard.

"Lobo y Melón used to play here," she once told me.

I've never experienced anything as exhausting as paternity. By eight in the evening I barely have the strength to drag myself to bed. What wears me out most isn't the work in itself, but the neurotic urge to imagine each and every thing my child is feeling and thinking.

Yesterday, while we were waiting by the large yellow door for the train to pass, I remembered the time Marisela and I were walking along the Coyuca Sand Bar. She was singing, from the depths of that dark night of language that is ignorance, a schmaltzy Spanish song: so you never forget me, not even for a moment, and we two live together in memories, so you never forget me. I'm a cynical, orphan ex-son of a whore who's read Saint John of the Cross: I know that the "tribe" won't give me words any purer than those unexceptional ones by Lorenzo Santamaría to explain to Leonardo, before I die, what it meant to me to eat ants by his side.

The death of Guadalupe Chávez and Marisela Acosta was a fast-forward version of her life.

In the first place, obstinacy: her death throes lasted from dawn to eleven at night.

Second, the comedy of errors: it took them eight hours to release her body because, when she was first admitted to the University Hospital a year before, someone had recorded her personal details incorrectly: they had rechristened her Guadalupe "Charles." A perfectly normal occurrence for my family. They had to make out the death certificate twice. What better homage could Mexican bureaucracy pay to a fugitive from her own name?

Third, the insult, the snide humor of violence. The man from the funeral parlor couldn't get the corpse into his hearse because there was a difference in height between the fender of his vehicle and the stretcher. He tried several times, pushing with all his might as if he were in a bumper car. The stretcher bounced against the fender, and the body of my defunct mother, wrapped from head to toe in a dirty sheet, wobbled like Jell-O. I felt a mixture of indignation, embarrassment for the man, and the desire to giggle. He, for his part, was ashamed and furious. I remembered something I'd once been told: "People have a word of honor; wild beasts don't." Finally, Saíd and I took pity on the contrite driver and helped him to load the bundle.

We didn't go in for any ceremony: we had her cremated, and that was that. For many years, since Jorge left home, I'd been given precise instructions.

"Here, Cachito," she said, drunk on rum and shame, going into the underground parking lot of a funeral parlor. "You bring me here and you burn me. Swear it."

"I swear, but let's go. Someone's going to complain."

"Swear it, Cachito. Don't let them bury me or make a big fuss. Quietly, without telling anyone, you come and you burn me."

At noon the ashes were handed over to us in a rectangular urn of fake pink marble.

Each one of us dealt with it in our own way. In Yokohama, Jorge set out walking in a straight line and didn't stop until the sea got in his way. Diana, who had shared the house with Guadalupe, had to take refuge in a hotel. Saíd, on the other hand, seemed illuminated by pain; I never saw him so somber.

What was delicious during those first days of mourning was the exact instant of waking: when it still hadn't dawned on me that my mother was dead, and I could enjoy the absence of the unrelieved anguish her suffering caused me for a year. But almost immediately, unhealthy lucidity would emerge: there is nothing more sinister than light.

And then Leonardo was born. Every abyss has its lullabies.

I don't remember when I saw her on her feet for the last time. I guess it was at the door to her house. She always used to accompany you to the door. It wasn't a matter of being polite, she was just garrulous: she talked nonstop. It was impossible to shut her up. You had to begin saying good-bye at least half an hour before you wanted to leave. In her own defense, she'd counter:

"It's your fault, you never come around. There's a lot to tell you."

The truth is she used to repeat the same thing eighty times. My whole life, I've detested the fact that she talked so much. Yet what made me hit the floor when the doctor came to inform me she'd finally died was the simple revelation that I'd never hear her voice again.

During the last week, we phoned each other every day: she wanted to be up-to-the-minute on everything happening around the birth. On September 9, at night, I heard a hacking cough on the other end of the line.

"Let's see the doctor."

"Yes," she said. "But we'll wait until morning. I've got an appointment for a checkup anyway."

Diana called at three in the morning to tell me they were leaving for the ER. Mónica and I met her there. Just before dawn, Saíd and Norma arrived too.

She was admitted into intensive care. Her platelets were

rock bottom and the fluid on her lungs, which had never been drained, was threatening to block her respiratory tract. It was no one's fault. She was simply broken: a year of virus and venom is too much for an organism whose only empire has been to assimilate every variety of blows.

At midday, they confirmed she did not have long to live.

"I suggest you say your good-byes," said Valencia. "It's a matter of hours."

My brother and sisters took it in turns to visit with her.

"Go home," I said when they had finished. "I'll let you know."

That was my role.

I waited until they all, including Mónica, had left the hospital. I needed to be alone: I couldn't have borne for anyone to touch me after going in to see her.

I went into intensive care. The nurse pointed to a cubicle on the left. I drew back the curtain. She was connected to more weaponry and little lights than ever. A transparent plastic mask covered her mouth and nose. She could no longer see.

There was nothing to say: we'd had a whole year of lucid pain.

In case you have any doubts, I did say it. I said:

"I love you. I'm my mother's son."

She was just about able to squeeze my hand. It was a squeeze of gratitude, without resignation, without pardon, without forgetting: merely a perfect reflection of panic. That was the last brick of education Guadalupe Chávez left to me. The most important of all.

Saltillo University Hospital,
October 2008 / Lamadrid, Coahuila, March 2011

Julián Herbert was born in Acapulco in 1971. He is a writer, musician, and teacher, and is the author of several poetry collections, a novel, and a story collection, as well as a book of reportage. He lives in Saltillo, Mexico.

Christina MacSweeney was awarded the 2016 Valle Inclán Translation Prize for her translation of Valeria Luiselli's *The Story of My Teeth*. She has published translations of two other books by the same author, and her translation of Daniel Saldaña París's novel *Among Strange Victims* was shortlisted for the 2017 Best Translated Book Award. She has also published translations, articles, and interviews on a wide variety of platforms and contributed to the anthologies *México20*; *Lunatics, Lovers & Poets: Twelve Stories after Cervantes and Shakespeare*; and *Crude Words: Contemporary Writing from Venezuela*.

The text of *Tomb Song* is set in Chaparral Pro. Created by type designer Carol Twombly, Chaparral is named for the drought-resistant shrubland on the arid coastal range near Twombly's California home. Book design by Ann Sudmeier. Composition by Bookmobile Design & Digital Publisher Services, Minneapolis, Minnesota. Manufactured by Friesens on acid-free, 100 percent postconsumer wastepaper.